THE GEEK'S GUIDE TO UNREQUITED Love

A NOVEL BY
SARVENAZ
TASH

SIMON & SCHUSTER BFYR
New York   London   Toronto   Sydney   New Delhi

Also by Sarvenaz Tash

THREE DAY SUMMER
THE MAPMAKER AND THE GHOST

SIMON & SCHUSTER BFYR
An imprint of Simon & Schuster Children's Publishing Division
1230 Avenue of the Americas, New York, New York 10020
SIMON & SCHUSTER BFYR is a trademark of Simon & Schuster, Inc.
For information about special discounts for bulk purchases, please contact Simon &
Schuster Special Sales at 1-866-506-1949 or business@simonandschuster.com.
The Simon & Schuster Speakers Bureau can bring authors to your live event. For
more information or to book an event, contact the Simon & Schuster Speakers
Bureau at 1-866-248-3049 or visit our website at www.simonspeakers.com.
Book design by Lucy Ruth Cummins
The text for this book was set in Adobe Garamond Pro.
Manufactured in the United States of America
First Edition
10 9 8 7 6 5 4 3 2 1
Library of Congress Cataloging-in-Publication Data
Names: Tash, Sarvenaz, author.
Title: The geek's guide to unrequited love / Sarvenaz Tash.
Description: First Edition. | New York : Simon & Schuster Books for Young Readers, [2016] |
Summary: Graham Posner is trying to get his best friend, Roxana, to fall in love with him by
planning the perfect weekend for her at Comic-Con.
Identifiers: LCCN 2015033511| ISBN 9781481456531 (hardback) |
ISBN 9781481456555 (eBook)
Subjects: | CYAC: Love—Fiction. | Friendship—Fiction. | BISAC: JUVENILE FICTION /
Social Issues / Friendship. | JUVENILE FICTION / Love & Romance. | JUVENILE
FICTION / Comics & Graphic Novels / General.
Classification: LCC PZ7.T2111324 Ge 2016 | DDC [Fic]—dc23 LC record available at
http://lccn.loc.gov/2015033511

To Amy and Katie, for befriending a geek
when it mattered most.

And to Bennett, for putting love
in a whole new stratosphere.

Chapter 1
WHEN A ONCE-IN-A-TIME-LORD-LIFETIME OPPORTUNITY PRESENTS ITSELF, SEIZE IT

"I KNOW WE'VE BEEN FRIENDS FOR SUCH A LONG TIME, ROXANA. I ONLY HAVE about five years' worth of memories without you in them. But . . ."

Here's where the next panel would come. And in an ideal world, I'd ask Roxy herself to help me figure it out. She would sketch something, sometimes just a ghost of a line, and on the best of days, a dying ember would ignite and suddenly I'd know exactly what came next. I need her. I need her to help me figure out how to tell her I love her.

I know what it has to feel like: epic. But also sweet. Like the romantic subplot of a superhero movie. Like that rainy, upside-down kiss in *Spider-Man.* But knowing what something is supposed to convey and actually getting it to do that is incredibly hard. Ask any writer.

My phone buzzes from my nightstand, a longer buzz than I'm used to. A phone call instead of a text? I see Roxana's hastily sketched self-portrait flash across my screen and feel an inexplicable panic flit across my stomach, blaring a run-on sentence like an LED display: Oh god something must be wrong if she's calling me is she dead she's dead or worse oh god she has a boyfriend now and they're getting married . . .

I try not to let this spigot of crazy flow out into my voice, but as it turns out, I don't get the chance to say anything.

"GrahamGrahamGraham, guess what? He's coming!" Her voice is completely out of breath, like my stepsister sounds after a track meet, and I have absolutely no idea what she's talking about. But I smile anyway. Probably one of the stars of the endless British TV shows she's always binge-watching is going to be in a Broadway play. I should check my bank account to see if I can afford a ticket anytime soon. I grab my iPad and hit the banking app.

"Who—" I start, but she doesn't let me finish.

"ROBERT ZINC."

I stop typing mid-password, stunned. "Coming?" Coming where? Surely not to Long Island. Or even anywhere in the eastern United States. Or anywhere at all that could be pinpointed on a map. Zinc hasn't been seen, interviewed, or photographed since November 3, 1995. Not even five years ago when the reboot of *The Chronicles of Althena* happened. Not even six months ago when the film adaptation was finally announced, cast, and actually shooting.

"To Comic Con. New York Comic Con. Go check the boards. Go check the boards now."

I zip over to my laptop and type in: *z-men.net*. First message of the forum, in capital letters, is exactly what Roxy has just told me.

I can't believe it. Robert Zinc, creator of my favorite series ever and the J. D. Salinger of the comic book world, is coming out of hiding. Has agreed to an exclusive forty-five-minute, *in-person* Q&A. And it's open to the public at New York Comic Con, taking place three weeks from now only an hourlong train ride away. Roxy and I already have passes for the weekend, only . . .

"It's on Friday," Roxana says, with an incredulous finality. "At three p.m." Her voice is flat.

"Don't you think your parents would let you skip school for this?" I urge. "This is once in a lifetime . . . not even once in a regular lifetime. Once in a Time Lord lifetime."

"Obviously. I know that. And *you* know that. But explaining it to Maman and Baba . . ." She takes in a deep breath. "But I will try. Oh, how I will try."

In the meantime, I've frantically clicked over to the NYCC website, even though I'm positive Friday passes have already sold out (they have). Fine, I'll take care of that later. Right now, I need to figure out how getting into the Q&A is going to work.

It's just three sentences: "Robert Zinc, creator of the once-cult

The Chronicles of Althena, will be sitting down for an incredibly rare Q&A with Solomon Pierce-Johnson, the director of the upcoming *The Chronicles of Althena* movie. This event will need exclusive wristbands that can be obtained Friday morning starting at 9 a.m. at the Javits Center. One wristband per attendee."

"Right," I say, my brain going into organizational overdrive. Once hologrammed thought projections become a reality, this will be the point at which a large spreadsheet will beam out of my forehead. "Nine a.m. tickets means we have to line up on Thursday night. Probably starting at nine p.m." I have personally never done this before, but I know, generally, how tickets to hot panels work. If they're handing them out first thing in the morning, the die-hard fans will line up as soon as the previous night's convention closes. And really, who is Comic Con made of if not boatloads of die-hard fans?

Roxy sighs, then laughs a little bitterly. "No problem, right? Not only can I cut school on Friday to go, but I'll definitely be allowed to spend Thursday hanging out on a street. In New York City. Overnight. This is the start to an amazing fantasy series." Roxy's parents are incredibly strict. She often chalks it up to them being, as she calls it, "maximum Persian."

"We'll figure it out, Roxy. I promise," I say fiercely, my brain spreadsheet starting a whole new tab for how to get Roxy to NYCC on Friday.

I hear her breathing relax a tiny bit and she laughs again, this time a little more freely. "All right, Graham," she says. "I don't know why, but I believe you."

I feel a jolt in my heart at her implicit trust in me, and then, suddenly, my virtual spreadsheet is a siren, flashing blue and red.

Comic Con? Robert Zinc? A weekend immersed in practically everything we love as individuals and together? This is it: the perfect opportunity to profess my unrequited love.

The spreadsheet explodes into confetti. Because maybe if the gesture is grand enough, and perfect enough, it won't be unrequited at all and *I*, Graham William Posner—lanky, pale, glasses, and with a penchant for fantasy worlds—will actually get the girl.

Chapter 2
EVERY GEEK HAS HIS PRICE

AS EXPECTED, I FIND FRIDAY TICKETS FOR NYCC ON EBAY, NO PROBLEM. WELL, other than the fact that Roxy and I may have cleared out most of our bank accounts for them. I want to insist on paying, to go along with my plan to sweep her off her feet, but she gives me a weird look when I suggest it, reminding me that it isn't her birthday or anything. I realize I have to play it cooler than that if I want to set this up right. I need to orchestrate it so that when the moment comes, she's surprised but, on the other hand, not so shocked that she completely loses it or anything. Kind of what my favorite book on writing says about how to end a story: make it unpredictable but also inevitable.

On Tuesday, I go over to her yard so we can have our weekly writing session. Most of the leaves on the trees are red and gold already, and the wind is getting crisper as September wanes, but we still have a few weeks left of sitting out comfortably on her deck, eating the fruit and nuts that her grandmother insists on bringing out to us. We don't get much work done today, though. We can't stop talking about what we'll ask Robert Zinc if there is somehow an open-mic Q&A at the end of his panel and we're lucky enough to get the chance to ask a question.

"How about 'Where do you get your ideas?'" I tease.

"Original," Roxana shoots back. "Not to mention, it's not like you don't already know the answer to that, since it's one of about twenty questions he ever answered."

I grin.

"'Where would Althena be right now?'" Roxana offers.

"Awesome one," I agree. "Though I feel like copper670 already wrote the answer to that." I've developed a theory that one of the z-men.net users is actually Zinc himself, incognito. He writes a lot of fan fiction that I've started recently calling just plain author fiction. It's that good, and it's completely in Zinc's style.

"Well, there's a question to ask him so that we can settle this debate once and for all. 'Are you copper670?'" Roxy slams her black marker down enthusiastically, leaving the panel she was working on half inked.

"But then what will you give me when I win?" I flash her a Cheshire cat grin.

She looks down at her sketchbook and runs her hand over the back of her hair. At the beginning of the summer, she took a picture of Mia Farrow in *Rosemary's Baby* to the salon and chopped off the waist-length hair she's always had. The cut accentuates her big eyes and long neck and is, plain and simple, stupidly hot, especially when she runs her hands through the buzzed part when she's thinking, which she does a lot during our writing sessions.

Now her lips purse to the side and she gets a mischievous gleam in her eye. "If you win, we can kill off Slammerghini."

I nearly gasp. Slammerghini is one of her favorite characters of ours to draw, but I've had a problem coming up with good story lines for him for years. There's only so many ways a mage can turn himself into a jail cell to catch the bad guys, you know?

"Or how about if I win . . ." What I want to say is, *I get to kiss you.* And there is a moment when everything gets suddenly quiet, except for a soft breeze that releases a flurry of maple leaves between us. I stare into her big brown eyes, gleaming copper and gold as they reflect autumn back at me. I almost reach my hand out to touch her buzzed chestnut hair. I almost cup her cheek and just lean in and do it. It's almost a perfect moment.

But then I don't. I freeze. I look away a moment too late, and then Roxana looks away too, puzzled. And instead of everything being perfect and romantic and aligned exactly right, it's awkward and askew, like we've just missed an important beat in the story. It's moments like this that make me wish life had second drafts.

"I think killing off Slammerghini is a pretty good deal, Posner. And if *I* win, we have to make a whole three-issue arc about him." She picks up her marker again and goes back to cross-hatching Rewinder's cape.

And just like that, the moment is gone forever.

I obsess about it all week, feeling like I've failed everything pop culture has ever taught me about romance by letting the opportunity slip out of my hands. But after I've sufficiently beat myself up over it (three full days), I allow it to fuel my fire to make Comic Con even more perfect for the two of us. I sit out in my yard, staring at the back of Roxana's fence—at the gate that I made my dad put in there when I was nine so that we could get in and out of each other's backyards easily—and scheme out every detail. I print out maps of the Javits Center and schedules of the events, and start a list that is unabashedly titled "Things Roxana Loves," with the goal of incorporating as many of the items into our weekend as possible. If things work out, by the end of New York Comic Con, my name will be on that list. I even reread all twenty-four issues of *The Chronicles of Althena* and take notes on all the most romantic bits—on all the perfect lines that Charlie Noth says to Althena as he falls for her. **"I have no idea what you really look like. But I still know you're the most beautiful thing I've never seen"** is a particular standout. Maybe I can incorporate an adaptation of that somehow.

On Friday morning, it's time to launch Phase 2 of the plan's centerpiece: the Robert Zinc panel. Before school, I bike over to my friend Casey Zucker's house. His parents are backing out of their driveway when I get there, on their way to their teaching jobs at Stony Brook University. I wave at them.

I find Casey up in his room, putting an enormous amount of white glop in his hair and running his hands through it until he's created vertical black spikes that would look right at home on a medieval mace. Casey discovered hair product about six months ago. I guesstimate another six months before he figures out he doesn't need to go through a bottle a week.

"NYCC. Zinc. Here's the deal." I don't waste time with preliminaries.

"Ugh. Don't even get me started, dude." He immediately goes over to his desk and hits a key on his computer to fire up the monitor. A spreadsheet fills the enormous display, each of its cells filled with minuscule font. "I had *everything* planned out weeks ago and the panel has messed up my entire schedule. I might even have to skip out on a Jim Lee signing *and* a Joss Whedon meet-and-greet."

"Or maybe," I say, leaning against his dresser and staring at his neat bookcase full of plastic-wrapped comic books, "you won't."

"It's not ideal," Casey continues. "I'll give you that. But . . . I do have to learn to be a little more flexible. I suppose." He sighs as he clicks on something on his spreadsheet and deletes it.

"*Or* you can just stick to your original plan that you've spent months perfecting," I counter again.

Casey finally turns around in his desk chair, one eyebrow raised. "All right. What's going on?"

That's the problem with having the class valedictorian as one of your best friends. It can be pretty hard to try and slide something by him.

"I have a proposal," I say. He continues to stare at me, and I know my best bet is to just be straight with him. "You stand in line with me to get the Robert Zinc wristbands, and then let me give your wristband to Roxana. In exchange"—Casey guffaws, but I don't let that deter me—"I will give you my pristine Issue Number One of *Giant-Size X-Men*."

We stare at each other across Casey's room. It's a good offer. Nay, it's a great offer. The issue was a gift from my dad and I checked its value just before coming over today. It's worth well over a grand these days.

"A, 'Pristine' is stretching it," he finally says. "It's an eight point five, tops."

Now it's my turn to guffaw. "Excuse me, but do I need to show you the paperwork again? This is a really interesting time for your photographic memory to fail you."

"B, you are insane," Casey says, ignoring me, "if you think I'd bail on seeing Zinc." He puts his computer to sleep and gets up to find his backpack.

I sigh. I really thought the *Giant-Size X-Men* offer would hold more water with him. "Okay, then, what do you want?"

"Nothing," Casey says without flinching. "I'm not missing Robert Zinc."

I watch him carefully put two textbooks into his bag and zip it. There's no way I'm ready to give up.

"There has to be something you'd miss him for," I say. Every geek has a price, something my dad, the OG—Original Geek—taught me long ago.

Casey's dark eyes stare into mine, and in a moment I'm pretty sure he's finally achieved his lifelong ambition of developing a mind-reading serum. Because he brings up the OG too. "Your dad's Obi-Wan figure."

For an insane moment, I actually consider it, and the notion that I can somehow get my hands on it, all heist-like, and then just *hand it over* to Casey. But this is real life, not *The Sandlot*.

"I'm inheriting that in about sixty years. Maybe come talk to me then." Even though I know I'll never give it up, even then. The 1978 double-telescoping Obi-Wan figure, untouched and in its original box, is my legacy. Not to mention, whenever I do get it, my dad's ghost would definitely haunt me were I to just give it away.

"How about . . ." I have a sudden flash of brilliance. "My full Legends Awakened set?" Value-wise, this has nothing on Obi-Wan, of course. But sentimentally, it was one of the few things Casey didn't own when we were kids, and he wanted it . . . bad. It just so happened that those Pokémon booster packs came out during one of the years when both of his parents were on sabbatical and working on their respective academic books. It was a good year for us to play video games and eat as much sugar as we wanted with zero to no parental supervision. A bad one for Casey to get a single birthday present he had asked for, partially because Mr. and Mrs. Zucker were too distracted and partially because money was pretty tight that year.

Casey brings his hands together and looks down into them, as if divining the answer there. I think I may have just hooked him and congratulate myself on my late-blooming genius. "And the *Giant-Size X-Men*?" he asks.

"Yes. Fine," I agree, feeling relieved that our negotiations are at an end.

Only, he pauses again, still examining his hands, which he's now rubbing together exactly like a cartoon villain.

"Come on, Case," I finally plead, trying to appeal to his heretofore nonexistent romantic side. He didn't seem particularly fazed when I told him a month ago that I was in love with Roxy. In fact, I think his exact reaction was to tell me that my lack of concentration was costing us the Warcraft raid. But I plunge on anyway. "I have to tell Roxy how I feel, and this is the perfect opportunity. You know how she feels about Robert Zinc."

His eyes narrow. "You know how *I* feel about Robert Zinc."

"And you know how *I* feel about Roxana . . ." I trail off. I should've known better. This line of beseeching isn't going to get anywhere with Casey.

Or so I think. "Okay, throw in one more thing and I'm in," he says, finally staring up at me again with a gleam in his eye.

I draw in a sharp breath. "What?"

"The *X-Men* Number One, Legends Awakened, and . . . get Callie to agree to a date with me."

My jaw nearly hits the floor. "Callie? Callie . . . McCullough?" I say numbly. As if we know any other Callies beside my stepsister.

"Yup," Casey says, swinging his backpack over his shoulder and heading for his bedroom door.

"Just how am I supposed to do that?"

Casey shrugs. "I leave the method up to you. But those are my terms. Take them or leave them."

I follow him out, stunned. Maybe I was wrong about Casey and romance after all. Maybe every geek not only has a price, but a girl who makes him crazy, too. As evidenced by the fact that he would even think to lump a date with a real-life person in the same category as some cards and a comic book (no matter how awesome they are). Maybe he's as far gone as me.

That's my own excuse, anyway, for immediately trying to figure out how to get my super-popular, athletic, senior stepsister to agree to a date with someone who, in her parlance, would inevitably be a junior dork. My mind churns for our entire way to school.

Chapter 3
PLANNING AND SCHEMING AND THINKING AND PRAYING

"WHAT, GRAHAM?" CALLIE GLARES AT ME OVER OUR BOXES OF CHINESE FOOD.
Her mom, Lauren, picked some up on the way home from her office.
My dad has only just gotten in about five minutes ago himself. Home-
cooked meals at the Posner/McCullough house are an extremely rare
occurrence, and the proximity of Number One Chinese Kitchen to
Lauren's office means my weekly diet consists of Shrimp Chow Fun
probably more than is good for my arteries.

"Nothing," I say as I stab some more of the greasy noodles with my
fork.

"Why do you keep staring at me?" She's still in her maroon soccer uniform, and her bright red hair clashes spectacularly with the jersey. "Are you in love with me or something?"

"Ewww," I say automatically. Technically, Callie and I aren't related, of course, but that would still be seriously gross.

Her brother, Drew, snickers next to her. Drew and I are in the same grade, and that's exactly where our similarities end. We've never even had a single class together, since I'm in honors everything and Drew . . . well, let's just say Drew plays football, lacrosse, and baseball proficiently, but he attends class a little less proficiently. I'm still not sure he's ever handed in a single stitch of homework, though, to be fair, I didn't know him before the fourth grade. Maybe he aced finger-painting and then decided that was enough of a scholarly peak for him.

I take it back. The McCulloughs and I do have one other thing in common: bizarrely, we all have red hair, though mine is a deeper auburn than theirs. When Dad and Lauren first got married, Roxana got a kick out of calling us the Weasleys, but within a few months she stopped because even a ten-year-old could tell that shared red hair does not a real family make.

I stare at the logo that decorates our takeout boxes. It's a number sign followed by a thumbs-up illustration, which is why Roxy and I always call the Chinese place Hashtag Like Restaurant. We've decided its slogan should be: An Eatery Ahead of Its Time.

Roxana. Robert Zinc. Casey. Callie. That seems to be the flowchart I'm stuck with. I have to make this work somehow.

SARVENAZ TASH

"I hung out with Casey today," I blurt to no one in particular, figuring maybe at least planting the seed of his name will be a start.

There's a long pause that my dad finally fills with, "How's he doing?"

Plotting how to get his hands on Obi-Wan, an evil part of me wants to respond, but I settle for "Good." And then struggle to follow that up with anything meaningful.

Dad nods and smiles. Nobody else registers that I've said anything.

"How was practice?" Lauren asks Callie and Drew.

"The new forward is really good," Callie says. "I think we're going to beat Harborfields this weekend without a problem."

"At least somebody will," Drew grumbles. "The lax team is bullshit this year."

"Watch the language, please," Lauren says mildly, which is pretty rich considering how many times we all hear her swear on her frequent after-hours conference calls.

I zone out, mentally starting to add items to my "Things Roxana Loves" list instead of listening to sports stats that literally mean nothing to me.

John Hughes movies
White chocolate Hershey's Kisses
Micron markers in all six nib sizes
Anything on BBC America

Robert Zinc

Robert Zinc

ROBERT. ZINC.

God, I really have to figure out a way to get this Callie/Casey thing to happen. The night is a total wash in that regard, but as far as I'm concerned, the deal with Casey is on. It has to be. Before bed, I put my *Giant-Size X-Men* and Pokémon deck aside on a high shelf in my closet, ready to hand them over as soon as NYCC ends. The important thing for now is that Casey knows I'm as good as my word and that I'll figure the Callie situation out . . . somehow. I wonder if I can bribe her by offering to trade rooms. She has complained about the size of her closet more than once, and mine is definitely bigger. I stare woefully at all my carefully stacked board games, video games, and boxes of comic books. Man, the things a geek will do in the name of love . . .

I don't see Casey much over the next week. This is the first year we actually don't share any classes, plus he's been preoccupied with preparing for the PSATs. Casey is gunning for a National Merit Scholarship. Stony Brook is a pretty good school and he could go there for free thanks to his parents' jobs, but Casey is a man with Ivy League dreams and always has been. I know he's determined to get all the scholarship money his freakishly enormous brain can finagle.

In the meantime, the other crucial part of the plan involves making sure Roxana can cut school on Comic Con Friday.

In my experience—by which I, of course, mean brainstorming plot-lines for *The Misfits of Mage High*—the simplest plans are often the best ones. And since this isn't a story I'm writing that needs obstacles thrown at it every five seconds to keep it interesting, I don't see why the simplest plan shouldn't just flat-out work.

Roxana will tell her parents she has school, followed by a dress rehearsal for the play, where the pit orchestra would of course need their star viola player. That will give her from 7 a.m. until about 7:30 p.m. to be away from home without anyone raising an eyebrow. But of course, instead of school, she'll be taking an early train into the city in the morning, having the most unforgettable day of her life, and then catching the 6 p.m. train back home.

"Easy peasy," I say as I spear a Tater Tot at our cafeteria table. We're going over our plan one more time. "But just remember to have the cab to the train station pick you up a few blocks over."

"Oh, no need for that." Felicia, Roxana's girl best friend, flips her long, silky black hair over her shoulder. "My brother said he'd drop us off at the station."

I stare at her. "Us?" I ask. There is no way Felicia Obayashi has any interest in Comic Con.

She grins back at me, gracefully piercing a piece of lettuce with her plastic fork. "You're getting Miss Goody-Two-Shoes here to cut class, lie to her parents, and spend a day in New York City? Of course I'm going to be there." She carefully flicks her wrist, and right before my eyes, her piece of lettuce folds and gets plopped into her mouth without smearing a jot of the shiny pink stuff she wears on her lips. I've suspected Felicia of practicing ninja mind tricks for years, and not just because she's of Japanese descent, either, but because I'm doubtful that there's a nonsupernatural way for someone to be so pretty, so smart, so talented, and so popular.

"Um . . . so you need tickets to get into Comic Con . . . ," I start.

Felicia looks at me with a pitying expression. "Duh. I don't know if you know this, Graham, but other people know how to use the Internet too. Anyway, I think it'll be fun to see Roxana all in her element. Plus hot guys in spandex, right? That might happen too?"

"Um, right." I shift uncomfortably on my bench. Not for one second have I expected that it would be anyone other than me and Roxana and occasionally Casey roaming the NYCC floor together. I don't know how having Felicia hanging around is going to work into my plans. I mean, I don't have a problem with her or anything. Felicia's just always been the mysterious wild-card element of Roxy's life for me. They've been stand partners in orchestra since the fourth grade, but she's always seemed one step ahead of Roxy socially and at least ten steps ahead of me. I know she's had several boyfriends already; I think she's gone to prom as both a freshman and a sophomore. There's a part of me that's always known that Roxana must confide stuff in her that she wouldn't tell me, as a guy. It never bothered me before this summer, though—when I realized that I didn't want to be just *a* guy, but I wanted to be *her* guy. Felicia must have some insight into that. The question is, would it be insight I want? Or is Roxana hopelessly in love with some jocky senior football player I could never be?

"Just don't forget," Roxana tells Felicia with a gleam in her eye, "there are also plenty of regular guys in spandex too. In fact, the ratio of hot to nonhot bodies in tight clothing might not be what the superhero movie industry has led you to believe." She plops the rest of her feta and cucumber pita sandwich in her mouth and grins at me.

"True," I say, smiling back at her. "Think more Chris Pratt and Seth Rogen before the personal trainers." I'm being paranoid. There's no way this girl is crushing on a high school cliché. I *know* this girl. And now a tiny piece of feta cheese is stuck at the corner of her mouth and I desperately want to reach over and brush it off.

But Felicia beats me to it by indicating the corner of her own mouth to Roxy. "Fair enough," she says. "But one thing's for sure, I am not missing out on Roxana Afsari's Day Off."

Roxana looks nervous but retorts with, "Well, now I know not to take my father's 1961 Ferrari, then."

"What are you talking about? We'll just run it in reverse to get the speedometer to turn back," I say.

"And hijinks will be sure to ensue." She crumples up her sandwich's tin foil and stares at it before looking back up at us. "Seriously, though, guys. Getting caught cutting and lying is not an option."

Felicia rolls her eyes. "We know. Relax." She elegantly places a cherry tomato into her mouth, chewing and swallowing it before continuing. "Graham would never let you get in trouble, so if he's planning it out, you know you're good."

Huh.

Felicia isn't looking at me, and she doesn't act like what she said means anything earth-shattering. But I'd be lying if I said I'm not a little flattered that she thinks that highly of me. Maybe she *does* know something that Roxy told her in confidence . . . and maybe it's something in my favor after all.

Chapter 4
GEEKS IN NEW YORK

THE GOOD THING ABOUT HAVING AN OG FOR A DAD IS THAT NOT ONLY WILL he allow you to take a day off from school to attend NYCC, but he'll even drop you off at the train station the day before to go spend your night standing on a line. Lauren may raise an eyebrow as she sees me and my enormous backpack standing in the front hallway at 7 p.m., but even she doesn't say anything except to "be careful." Callie tells me to try and avoid being trampled by a nerd stampede, but I doubt she'd be too concerned were that to actually happen. Drew just blinks blankly at me and then dismisses me from his mind as he goes back to texting what is likely some grammatical atrocity to his girlfriend.

Casey's parents are pretty hands-off when it comes to this sort of stuff, probably because they know their son is way more anal about his schoolwork than even they would be. I know he's prepared as much as possible for his day off from school by speaking to all of his teachers and getting his homework done ahead of time. Which is why I can't figure out why he seems so distracted on the car ride to the station. He barely says two words to me or to my dad, even after Dad asks him if he'd mind getting Peter Mayhew's autograph on his behalf. Dad ends up giving me the cash for the autograph, along with the photo he wants signed: a two-shot of Chewbacca and Han Solo.

We buy our tickets, board the LIRR, and sit at the end of the car where the red and blue seats face each other. We're going against the rush-hour crowd, most of whom are heading home from their city jobs, so the train is pretty empty. I wait until we've passed a few stops before I hand the Mayhew photo over to Casey and finally break the silence. "So, what's up, Case?"

"What?" Casey responds, barely even looking at me.

"Oh, nothing," I say. "Just that you've been planning this weekend for the past six months and you look as excited as you would going to a pep rally. So what's up? What happened?"

He sighs into his window, his breath depositing a small blotch of condensation. "I had an appointment with my guidance counselor today," he mutters.

"Yeah?" I'm confused. I can't imagine Casey ever having the bad kind of guidance counselor appointment. It's not like he's ever been in trouble. Seriously, not ever. Not even a mistaken cut slip or attendance snafu.

"You know . . . where they told us our class ranking."

"Oh, right," I say. I had mine yesterday, and so did Roxana. Mrs. Buchanan told me I'm currently sitting at number eleven in our junior class. Roxana is at number nine. She had a grand old time teasing me about being two places ahead of me on our bus ride home, mostly by repeating "Number nine, number nine, number nine" in a loop à la the Beatles. Casey has to be at number one . . . wait, doesn't he? I look over at him, and suddenly everything clicks into place. "You're not . . ."

He shakes his head, then takes his finger and writes the number two in the fog on his window.

"Whoa," I say, stunned. "So then who's number one?"

"No idea." Casey turns to me, his thick eyebrows fixed into a scowl. "Benji Conners? Ethan Kramer? I don't even know how it's possible. My average is 102.1."

I whistle. Casey takes so many honors and AP classes, one even in his sophomore year, that they get weighted to give him an above-perfect average. Ironically, I know having over a 100 percent average is something that bothers his math-wired brain, especially since any expression that involves someone giving, for example, 110 percent will really get him riled up.

I don't even attempt to tell Casey that this means he's still the salutatorian, or that he'll still probably get into any Ivy League school he wants. Casey Zucker is nothing if not a perfectionist. The things he cares about, namely academics, he's deeply interested in being the best at. One time he even told me he thought it was a shame that he didn't have an athletic bone in his body: that kind of fierce competitiveness could only come in handy on a field. It certainly doesn't hurt him during our Friday-night Magic tournaments.

"There's still time to change your ranking," I say, knowing it's the only thing he'll want to hear.

He nods ferociously. "Oh, yes. But first I have to find out who's number one so that I can strategize properly. Buchanan wouldn't tell me," he adds darkly.

After a few more minutes of brooding, I mention that I've talked Casey up to Callie over the whole week. What I neglect to mention is that this has mostly involved me bringing his name up once or twice during dinner, with no reaction from her. But no reaction is better than a negative reaction, right? Plus I think baby steps is definitely the way to go here. Or at least, that's what I tell myself, as my plans to make this date happen have yet to materialize beyond such infantile, minuscule, microscopic steps.

Still, Casey seems to be in slightly better spirits by the time we get to Penn Station, maybe because his mind has already started churning with a solution for the valedictorian problem. Once we've elbowed our way outside, we double-check Google maps to make sure we're headed in the right direction and then start the long, straight walk from Seventh Avenue to Eleventh Avenue.

We see lots of tourists with cameras and shopping bags, and some harried-looking New Yorkers in suits and ties. A group of college-age girls in tiny skirts and high, high heels wait with us at the corner of Eighth Avenue while the light changes.

At Ninth Avenue, we see our first Spider-Man and then, like he's heralded the cavalry, a steady stream of costumed people with badges around their necks are following him, heading in the opposite direction from us. By the time we get to Tenth Avenue, there are flushed faces and spandex as far as the eye can see, accompanied by excited chatter about the day's experiences. I can see Casey visibly relax. These are our people.

"Next year, we definitely have to try to be here for Thursday," I say.

"Especially if I've gotten in early decision," Casey agrees. "Senioritis, here I come."

I snort. Senioritis for Casey will probably mean exactly that: cutting one extra day to attend New York Comic Con.

As we get closer to the Javits Center, I start to see that more and more of our spandexed brethren haven't come here alone. In fact, a lot are coupled up, holding hands with significant others, laughing together, secure and happy in a geektastic world all their own. I want that to be Roxana and me so badly. I pull on the straps of my backpack and stand up a little straighter. This is my shot to make it happen, and I'll have to rise to the occasion to the best of my powers. *My sadly human powers,* I think as I spot a Wolverine and Jean Grey play-fighting each other, each with one set of Wolverine's claws.

The organizers will be giving out the Robert Zinc wristbands from this building at 9 a.m. tomorrow morning. Tucked away to the side of the front door, I start to see a snake of people who've made themselves comfortable there. Some have chairs, blankets, and even tents, and most are sitting down. I take a deep breath. There was a small part of me that thought maybe we'd be two of the first people in line, but if this is the Zinc line, and I'm growing more and more certain it is, based on the costumes I'm seeing, we aren't. Not by a long shot.

"Robert Zinc?" I ask a boy clad in a holey black shirt and wearing a faded mustard-yellow leather jacket, even though I already know the answer. He's dressed as Charlie Noth, the down-and-out sci-fi writer who meets the mysterious alien Althena in *The Chronicles of Althena.*

"Yes indeed," he tells me. I nod and then start the trek past the line that's winding its way around the building, my heartbeat pounding louder with every person we pass. What if we camp out here all night . . . and still miss out on getting a wristband?

concrete. It's cold here on the edge of Manhattan, where a wind that holds promises of a New York winter is blowing off the Hudson River. I've already put my extra sweatshirt on. Casey, who rarely gets cold himself, probably due to the insulating dark body hair that covers about 95 percent of his body, is still in a T-shirt.

He takes out a deck of cards and I'm surprised to see that they're regular playing cards, instead of his usual Magic deck. "Poker?" he asks.

I eye him warily. "Really?"

"I'm trying to broaden our horizons. See how the other half lives," he responds as he shuffles.

I shrug my assent and he deals. A few minutes in, I've flipped over a queen of spades in the river and I have to point out, "It's kind of boring without some epic backstory for her, isn't it?"

Casey squints at the card. "Maybe she's really a sorceress disguised as a queen?"

I look at her pointy staff and complicated cloak. "No disguise. Her subjects know she's a sorceress." I consider her again. "What they don't know is that the king and jack of spades are merely her puppets, created by her to give the illusion of a monarchy instead of a totalitarian state."

"Not bad," Casey says as he ups the ante by throwing in a couple more quarters.

We each win one hand but quickly get bored with the straight-forward game, moving on to a diversion that's much more our speed.

"Who would win in a fight," I start out, "a polar bear or a shark?"

Chapter 5
NERDLAM

"A HUNDRED AND TWO," CASEY SAYS AS HE COMES BACK TO JOIN ME AT THE square foot of brick wall that will be our companion for the night. He just went ahead and counted how many people are in front of us on line.

I breathe a sigh of relief. "I'm sure the hall holds at least two hundred and fifty."

"Definitely," Casey agrees.

I've taken out my sleeping bag, but it's still folded up and currently acting as a cushion beneath me. Casey takes his out of his backpack and places it next to me, making himself as comfortable as possible on the

"What's the playing field? Are they on land?" Casey responds, munching on a banana as his midnight snack.

"Well, no, the shark can't be on land."

"And the polar bear can't be underwater for that long."

"But he can be swimming. So they're both in the water."

Casey thinks for a second. "Polar bear. He has the sheer mass."

"Ah!" I retort. "But the shark can attack from underneath and move much quicker."

"Well, that's why I asked if they were on land! What if the polar bear was on an ice cap and the shark was circling it? Then the bear would have the upper ground and be able to swat at the shark with his massive paws."

"Maybe," I concede. "Until the shark rammed the ice cap, causing the bear to fall in the water. Bear is discombobulated, shark takes advantage. The end."

"Dude, how much force would it take for a shark to ram his face into an ice cap and cause a polar bear to fall off? He'd break his jaw first!" Casey finishes his banana, gets up, and goes to the street corner to dispose of the peel in a trash can.

"I got one!" he says as soon as he returns. "Who would win in a fight: Sean Bean as Boromir or Sean Bean as Ned Stark?"

"You mean which Sean Bean would die first and who would bite it second?" I retort, before giving it some thought. "Boromir was a noble man who fought many wars."

"As was Ned Stark," Casey points out as he unfolds his sleeping bag. Setting his backpack at one end, he stretches out, using his pack as a pillow.

"But he's a captain-general, commanding an entire army."

"I'm talking mano a mano here."

"Fine. He still has more combat experience. Day in and day out, he's thinking of battle strategy."

"Ned has a Valyrian steel sword."

"Ice?" I ask. "Come on. That's ceremonial. No way he would be using that in battle."

"And what if the ring is nearby. Can Boromir resist that?"

"Nuh-uh," I counter. "If it's mano a mano, there's no one else around. Your rules."

"I still think you're underestimating Ned."

I think about this for a second. "Maybe in a world of two Sean Beans, they both die at the exact same moment. Maybe it's like crossing the streams."

"Hmph," Casey says. "Maybe. Doubtless, it would be well matched."

"Indeed," I concede. I unfold my sleeping bag too, following Casey's lead by putting my backpack under my head. It's probably a good idea to keep our stuff as close to us as possible. A queue of Comic Con supernerds would probably be an easy mark for an enterprising pickpocket.

We play the game for a little while longer, debating the tenth

Doctor vs. the eleventh Doctor, Kirk vs. Picard, and Dumbledore vs. Gandalf. Eventually, Casey drifts off to sleep and I'm left alone with my thoughts, which inevitably land right on Roxana. I chose Dumbledore over Gandalf for sentimental reasons because the two of us bonded over the Harry Potter books first of all.

Dad and I lasted six months in our old house after Mom died. I think that was about all he could take of seeing the places where she used to cook, and laugh, and live—places that were then tainted with memories of her napping, and sleeping, and dying. He thought moving was the only thing to do, but I was terrified of going to a place that had never held her in it, worried that I would stop being able to picture her if we didn't have the same walls and floors as background. Unfortunately, there's only so much resistance an eight-year-old can possibly put up. Before I knew it, we were unpacking in a strange, big house that was miles away from Casey. We wouldn't even be going to the same elementary school anymore.

As I helped bring in box after box across our back patio, I saw a pair of dark eyes staring at me through the back fence. I didn't think anything of it until the owner of the dark eyes spoke to me.

"Which house do you think you'd be sorted into?" she asked, without introduction or preamble. The fence now came up to her chin, so she must have procured a stool to stand on. She held a hardcover copy of *Harry Potter and the Sorcerer's Stone* in her hand, and she smiled at me. It was probably the first time in months that someone had smiled at me without then telling me how sorry they were for me, either with their words or with their eyes.

"I've only read the first one," I admitted. "I don't know if I'm qualified to guess." I didn't tell her why I'd only read the first one. That Mom and I started reading them together right before her diagnosis and by the time we got to the end of *Sorcerer's Stone*, she was too sick to keep going. That I'd stopped myself from reading on without her, like some sort of bargaining chip with a literary god. Thinking if only we still had the rest of the series to read together, she couldn't die. That my mom, the story lover, couldn't leave without us finding out what happened.

"I'm not allowed to read past three yet," the girl continued. "But I think you know enough to pick your house after the first one, don't you?"

I stared at her. Her long, dark hair was flying all around the fence posts like Jolly Roger flags. "Ravenclaw," I finally said. "I think that's where I would be."

She broke out into a huge grin. "Me too! See, everybody always says Gryffindor just because that's the one Harry is in, but they don't pay attention to the qualifications. I'm Roxana, by the way."

"Graham," I said, only then realizing that it was kind of weird to be having a conversation with a girl my own age. I couldn't remember ever having one that long before.

"Do you want to read the books together? That way you can get caught up to where I am, at least."

"Okay," I said, and was immediately surprised at my own lack of hesitation. I should have been worried about how this would feel, about whether I would get sad thinking about my mom.

But before I had a chance to reconsider, Roxana spoke. "Be right over," she said. "Oh, if that's okay?" She looked worried for a second. "My mom says I need to learn how to ask permission better."

"That's okay," I said. With a swish of her long hair, Roxana left the fence and headed through her yard and inside her house. About a minute later I heard a knock at my own front door.

And then everything happened just like she said. We read the books together. We read many books together, mostly fantasy series. We grew up in each other's yards, in each other's lives. And to this day, I don't know what would have happened if she hadn't been there when my dad suddenly announced he was remarrying and then the McCulloughs moved in with us. It was a big change for a ten-year-old boy with a widowed parent, but I took it relatively in stride. Roxy made it easy to.

She makes everything feel easy. Everything except this new, scary feeling that has settled into me over the past few months. Suddenly I want more. I want to touch her, to feel connected to her by something more than friendship. I want to feel her lips with mine. I've never even had a real kiss before, one that wasn't on a nursery school playground anyway, and there's only one girl I can imagine having a meaningful one with: my writing partner and my best friend.

I fall asleep thinking of her and at 7:30 a.m., when my watch goes off, I wake up remembering I just dreamt about her.

Casey is up too, and he goes to scare us up a bagel from a nearby food cart. I stand and stretch, my back stiff and sore. I reach around and rub my own shoulder blades as I look at the people around us.

The line stretches far, far back behind us now. I can't even see the end. Despite the number of people, it's pretty quiet on the street. All I hear is the flat monotone of some guy who's saying, "Zinc *is* considerably overrated in my opinion, though. The series totally drops off after Issue Thirteen."

I cast an annoyed look at the line and glimpse the culprit: some hulking guy in his thirties with mirrored sunglasses and a faded yellow trucker hat with Papa Smurf on it. He's now loudly going off about how the subplot with Althena's ex-lover who remains on her home planet— basically the antagonist of the series—is totally unnecessary. He is com- pletely and utterly wrong, obviously. Casey comes back with a sesame bagel and a raised eyebrow when he hears the tail end of this rant.

"Dude, I know," I acknowledge.

But a few more poorly constructed arguments later and even that guy seems to have run out of things to say. Maybe it's just the early hour, but the near silence that settles in is heavy with tension, like we're all waiting for a starting gun. Casey and I both eat without saying much.

We roll up our sleeping bags and pack up our backpacks and then we wait, shifting from one foot to the other. I think about the cos- tume in my bag, and I'm itching to get inside and put it on. So far, I haven't seen anyone on this line with my version of Althena.

"Hi, guys!"

It's Roxana and Felicia. I grin and let out a sigh of relief I didn't know I was holding.

"You made it!" I say, glancing at my watch. It's eight thirty in the morning. "No suspicion from the Afsaris?" I ask Roxana.

"In the clear, so far," Roxana says. "How was your night?"

"Cold and hard," Casey responds.

"Nah, it wasn't too bad," I immediately say when I see Roxy's eyes go big with concern.

"Hey, no cutting in line!" a gruff voice interrupts. We turn around to see some skinny middle-aged guy glaring at Roxana and Felicia. Felicia flashes him her best megawatt smile.

"We're not cutting," she says sweetly. "We're just hanging out with them until you guys get moving."

The guy continues to scowl. "Hang out with them once the floor opens. We've all been sleeping out here all night and you can't just barge in now."

"Right. Like I said . . . ," Felicia starts again stubbornly, but Roxana gently touches her arm and mutters something about Felicia not wanting to mess with early-morning nerditude.

Louder, Roxana says, "Never mind. We'll go stand on the entrance line and meet you guys inside, okay? Right by the front doors."

I nod. "Hopefully it won't take too long to get the wristbands."

"We'll wait," Roxana says, before she grabs Felicia's wrist and firmly leads her away to a different line around the other side of the building.

Felicia looked just about ready to continue her war of words with our grumpy neighbor.

A few minutes later, we can hear a faint voice shouting instructions from the front of the line. We strain to hear it, and I'm standing on my tiptoes, as if suddenly being an inch taller than six feet will allow me to see over the head of 102 people.

Everyone directly ahead of and behind me is muttering a variation of "What? What did he say?" People start to move, and we're all looking ahead, hoping the instructions will trickle down from our neighbors.

"Ah, our badges," Casey finally says when he catches a few people ahead of us putting their laminated Comic Con tickets over their heads.

I nod and kneel down to open my backpack. And in that one moment, everything changes.

I hear a big glass door creaking open; I feel the pounding of hundreds of feet around me. It's like that imaginary starting gun has gone off. Only, by the time I look up, I've missed it. I stand there like an idiot, my mouth agape as people *from all around me* rush to the doors.

"Oh my God," Casey says. We grab our backpacks and run too, but we're clearly a second too late on the uptake.

From behind a sea of people, I can just catch a glimpse of a bewildered NYCC employee standing at the door, shouting something that can't be heard. People are squeezing past him—including, I can't help but notice, Papa Smurf—and the employee turns around and calls after them, but he clearly can't leave his spot to chase them because of the crowd jostling for entrance in front of him. Not that he's much of a deterrent.

In a few moments, some other guys in teal staff T-shirts have come out and are trying to herd the crowd of people back into a line.

"Against the wall, against the wall. Back into the line now," one of them yells as he comes near us and uses his arms to prod us back into some sort of formation.

Eventually, Casey and I are back on a line, but we're nowhere near as close to the front as we were before. A continent of people stands between us and the door. I look around desperately, trying to see if I can find Grumpy Geek or anyone else who was near us in line before to vouch for our place. But I recognize no one.

The staff members are still calling for order, but they're turning a deaf ear to the onslaught of nerd rage that is suddenly being directed at them. Probably a job requirement.

Casey and I stare at each other, unable to believe what has just happened. I'm bewildered and I'm terrified. And then, twenty minutes later, I'm devastated.

There are about forty people ahead of us when we get the news. The wristbands are gone.

We will not see Robert Zinc today. I will not be able to take Roxy directly from meeting her favorite artist to a secluded corner of the Javits Center to tell her those three little words.

Everything is ruined.

Chapter 6
HIDEOUS PLANS BROUGHT TO YOU BY PLEBES

"I'M SORRY," I BLURT OUT. ROXANA LOOKS CRESTFALLEN, AND THERE'S NO WAY my face isn't reflecting her exact feelings right now—probably multiplied. "So sorry."

Her face softens a little. "Graham, it's not your fault. You slept on concrete last night, for chrissakes."

"You're damn right," Casey interjects loudly. "I cannot believe those . . . *assholes*. How is that okay? How? And can they really live with themselves knowing they stole something from its rightful owners? Is that the type of person whom Robert Zinc would even want in his audience?" I recognize the beginnings of righteous nerd wrath, but I'm too destroyed myself to try and stop him from having a full-blown rant in the middle of the Javits Center.

"That sucks," Felicia says in solidarity, though she's clearly the only one of us who is not genuinely about to have a nervous breakdown because Robert Zinc is in the building and we can't see him.

"Maybe we can find a way to sneak into the panel later," I say half-heartedly.

"Yeah. Maybe," Roxana says with a weak smile. She knows as well as I do that that's probably going to be impossible. New York Comic Con is usually a well-oiled machine, and this snafu should alert the organizers to the fact that they need to monitor the Zinc panel extra carefully.

"Well, look, this is still Roxana's big cut day. So let's go put on our costumes," Felicia says, lifting up and shaking her tote bag. "And then I have a surprise for us at eleven o'clock."

I'm so taken aback by the first part of her statement that I barely even register the second part. "Wait, you brought a costume?" I ask.

"When at Comic Con . . ." She smiles. "Besides, I look great in this."

Casey eyes her incredulously.

"The bathrooms are down these escalators," I say, leading the way. We split when we get to the men's and ladies' rooms, but Casey doesn't go in with me. "No costume this year," he explains.

Now it's my turn to look incredulous. "You're telling me that Felicia Obayashi is going to be walking around NYCC in a costume and Casey Zucker won't be?"

"My schedule is too intense, and I calculated that the costume would just get in the way, factoring in both the aerodynamics of maneuvering through the crowds and people stopping to talk to me or take my picture." He looks at his watch. "Speaking of which, the Lacey Grotowski signing starts in twenty minutes."

"I'll come with you to that," I say firmly. "And I think Roxana wants to get a sketch from her. I'll be out quickly."

I duck into a thankfully empty stall and make quick work of putting on my costume. I'm going to be one of the versions of Althena, Zinc's shape-shifting alien, who was inspired by Althena's eighties sci-fi movie marathon. I'm Mad Max, and yes, I am wearing black pleather pants. I bought them from Hot Topic, and though they are a little tough to tug on, I don't think they actually look too bad on me. I may have even tried a tongue-out, devil's-horns-up full rocker pose in the store's fitting room mirror when I first tried them on. I'm sure I gave some bored security guard a laugh.

After the pants, I put on a belt, a black leather jacket with one sleeve, and a cheap leg brace I bought off the Internet. Then I head out of the stall to take a look at myself in the mirror.

Not bad. The only thing I need to differentiate me from Mel Gibson's character—besides about fifty pounds of muscle—is a sea-green left earlobe. It's the only part of Althena she's unable to change, where she keeps her selfness, no matter whom she looks like. I dab some makeup on my ear, give myself a final once-over in the mirror, and head out.

The girls still aren't out, of course, and Casey is frowning at his watch. I'm about to tell him not to worry about the time, that Roxana is just as anxious as he is to see as much as possible, when she reappears and makes it a moot point.

I grin as soon as I see Roxy, the first time I've felt compelled to do so since we lost out on the wristbands. I don't know how she managed to do it in so short a time, but Roxana is dressed as one of the most famous iterations of Althena, the one she takes on when Charlie Noth meets her in the very first issue. Roxy has on a shaggy blond wig, a short black dress with mesh sleeves, sheer black holey leggings, and a beaded choker. She's painted a thick black rectangle across her eyes, like a bandit's mask, and her left earlobe is, of course, green. Althena came to Earth having seen snippets of *Blade Runner* growing up and being told that Daryl Hannah's replicant character was what humans dressed like. Luckily, she arrived on Halloween and was merely congratulated on her pitch-perfect costume by most people, including the instantly smitten Charlie Noth. And the rest was twenty-four issues of perfection. Just like the perfect girl standing in front of me now.

"'Uh, h-hello. Hi. Greetings. H-hi,'" I stammer.

Roxy grins as she recognizes the first line of dialogue Charlie ever says to Althena, but I'd be lying if I said I wasn't using Charlie's slack-jawed admiration to mask my own. Roxana looks phenomenal.

"'Salutations. Good evening. Nice to meetcha.'" She provides Althena's next line. "Great costume." That one is her own as she looks me over.

"You too."

"Ready?" Felicia says as she comes bounding out of the bathroom; she's dressed like Wonder Woman. I should have expected that.

"To Lacey?" Roxana asks.

"Let's do it," I respond as we head toward Artist Alley.

"Just don't forget. At eleven, we all have to follow me," Felicia chirps, jauntily striding across the floor in her small, patriotic shorts and knee-high red boots.

"What?" I ask. I have no idea what she could possibly be talking about.

"I signed us all up for something. It's a surprise," she says. "So we can go stand in line for whosy-whatsit to sign whatever right now, but at eleven, you're all mine for an hour."

Casey gawks at her back, and I already know exactly what he's thinking: that Felicia, for all her smarts and her charm, is completely out of her mind if she thinks she has any pull over his deeply thought-out schedule.

Regardless, we all get in line for Lacey Grotowski's signing, and it takes about forty minutes before we reach the front. Casey purchases the first issue of Lacey's new series and gets it signed. "Is it any good?" he asks Lacey cluelessly as he gives it to her.

She looks at him archly, but smiles. "Hope so," she replies gamely as she signs her name on the cover with a gold pen. Casey just nods.

When it's Roxana's turn, she also buys the first issue and then whips out a big red sketchbook from her backpack. "Would I be able to purchase a sketch from you?"

"Of course," Lacey responds, taking the book. "What did you have in mind?"

"Althena," Roxana responds.

Lacey starts flipping through the book and sees the dozen or so other sketches that Roxana has already collected, all from different artists, all different iterations of Althena.

"Niiice!" Lacey says. She points to a section of her right arm, which has a full sleeve tattoo proudly on display, and taps at a stylized *E* immersed in what looks like a fishbowl. It's the emblem for Althena's planet, Ezula. "You picked the right girl for the job."

Roxana smiles. "Oh, I know," she says before secretly glancing over at me. I know she's dying to get an Althena tattoo herself the minute she turns eighteen and doesn't need parental permission.

"Are you guys going to see Zinc later?" Lacey asks, and my heart sinks, the catastrophe in the forefront of my mind again. Without even realizing it, I glance over to a far corner of Artist Alley, where my map of the Javits holds a red heart in lieu of an *X*. That was supposed to mark the spot where I professed everything to Roxy. I swallow hard.

"We were supposed to," Casey answers for us darkly. "But then a bunch of jerks had no respect for the line we staked out all night."

"Ugh, that sucks!" Lacey responds. "I hate when shit like that happens."

Casey nods.

"I won't be able to go either, unfortunately. I have another sign-ing scheduled just at that time." She turns to Roxana and taps on the sketchbook. "Any particular version of Althena?" Lacey asks as she takes a Post-it and writes Althena's name on it.

"Artist's choice," Roxana says.

"Awesome," Lacey says. "I'll make it a good one, I promise. Pencil, ink, or color?" She points to the side, where there's a price list for her sketches: $30 for pencil, $50 for inked, and $80 for full color.

Roxana hesitates for a moment but then responds firmly. "Let's go with inked."

Lacey jots it down. "Is it okay for you to pick the book back up at four?"

"Definitely. Thanks!" Roxana says as we all leave Lacey's table.

"Perfect timing," Felicia says as she glances at her watch. "Follow me, guys."

"Felicia, where—" Roxana starts, but Felicia doesn't give her a chance to continue. She forges ahead and gets swallowed by a large mass of people. Roxana immediately hurries to catch up to her, and I have no choice but to follow them. Casey mumbles something about heading in that direction anyway as he falls into step beside me.

We weave our way through superheroes, wizards, and mustachioed plumbers as we go to the escalators and head down one level. Then Felicia swooshes down a long hallway, at the end of which I know some panels are taking place. What kind of Comic Con panel could Felicia possibly be interested in—Advanced Techniques in Hair Braiding? How to Match Your Eye Shadow to Your Cape?

I admit I'm curious as we advance toward the rooms in the back, but then we suddenly stop short in the middle of the hallway.

"Here we are," Felicia announces, pointing to a sign next to a set of double doors.

It reads: SPEED DATING.

"I read about it online, and I signed us all up," Felicia says brightly as she leads us to the back of the long line of people waiting outside the doors.

I laugh and turn to look at Roxana, waiting for her to guffaw with me. But instead, I see her looking carefully at the people in the line. As if she's checking them all out.

"Um, Felicia," I say, panic starting to set in, "you can't be serious."

"Won't it be fun?" Felicia responds, either not getting my tone or choosing to ignore it.

"Definitely a fun idea," Roxana says. "Nice job, Felicia." Roxana grins at her.

I stare at Roxana agape, and then I turn to Casey, my ally. Obviously, we are not doing this, and maybe he can help me find an excuse in his schedule for Roxana to not do this either.

But I see Casey looking rather intently at the line and a short red-headed girl dressed like Princess Zelda. Jesus, what is it with him and redheads?

As he's about to get on the end of the line without protest, I finally turn to Felicia. "Felicia, there is no way you want to date any of these people," I say, indicating the costumed crowd surrounding us, "is there?"

Felicia takes a good, hard look, and for a second, I think she might actually be reconsidering. But then she just smiles. "Why not? Maybe it's time I broaden my horizons. Roxana is always telling me to go for a nerd," she says playfully. "She says they're nice and they'll treat me well."

Really? Roxana said that?

But that couldn't have been in relation to me, right? Otherwise, Felicia wouldn't be bringing her here to meet *other* nerds.

Maybe spending the past few weeks chickening out from discussing this further with Felicia was not in my best interest after all.

But as the line starts to move with all of us on it, I realize that it's too late to do anything about that now.

Chapter 7
SPEED HATING

A GIRL WITH A CLIPBOARD HAS COME OVER AND CHECKED OFF OUR NAMES. WE are now all headed inside the giant conference room and being herded to one side, where a white piece of copy paper with the word *Teens* on it is stuck on the wall. There are rows and rows of large cafeteria tables with their attached benches set up in the room.

This is really happening.

I glance nervously over at Roxy and she grins nervously back at me.

"Looks kinda like the Great Hall at Hogwarts," she says, indicating the tables.

I nod. And, for a mad second, I wonder if this will somehow let me speed date her. Can I take those three minutes to tell her how I feel? Is this how it was meant to happen? And did Felicia, like, mastermind it that way?

Within a moment, my hopes are dashed. The girl who checked our names off is splitting us up into color-coordinated groups. I'm orange, Roxana is purple, Casey and Felicia are both blue. There are about six teen groups in all, two of them for same-sex couples and the rest for boy-girl pairings. We get escorted to our respective tables, and I begrudgingly sit down on the boys' side. Roxana is clear across the room. She's facing me, and all I can see are the backs of the guys who are about to get a chance to talk to her *on a date.* Because that's what this is. It's right there in the title.

I stare at the orange cutout heart that's decorating the middle of my table, and I almost wish I could take it and replace my own with it. Being in love is so complicated, I don't think I ever fully realized how insane and intense it can make everything feel—and not necessarily in a good way. **"Like punching a brick wall with your heart in your fist. Bloody. Messy. Painful"** is how Charlie Noth once described it.

A minute later, a serious-looking girl with magenta-rimmed glasses and a purple streak in her hair sits down in front of me. She's clutching a small packet of papers to her chest and studying it intently.

"Okay, folks. This is how this is going to work." The girl with the clipboard is standing in front of a microphone and what looks like a large ceremonial gong. "There are twenty people for everyone to meet today within each group. You get three minutes with each person. When you hear the gong, everyone on the left side of the table is going to slide down one place to their right. Three minutes. And then gong. Rinse and repeat for the full hour. Everyone got it?"

Her question is met with a nervous silence, which seems to satisfy her. "There are paper and pencils in the middle in case anyone wants to exchange information at the end of your dates. And now, let's make some love matches!" She takes a mallet and hits the center of the gong, which reverberates with its unmistakable sound.

Immediately, the room is filled with an uproar of chatter.

"Okay, first of all, *My Little Pony*," the girl in front of me says brusquely. "Thoughts?"

"Um . . ."

"Do you watch it?" she asks quickly.

"Uh . . . I've seen a few episodes," I reply. Which is true. I was curious about the cult aspect of it.

"How many is a few?" she asks, her eyes narrowing.

"Like . . . three. Maybe?"

She bristles, looks at the top sheet of her papers, flips it over, studies the second sheet, and then looks back up at me.

"So do you even know the characters?"

"You mean by name?"

"Name, appearance, function in Ponyville, et cetera."

"Um . . . isn't one of them Sparkle . . . something?" I attempt.

She shakes her head. "Right. So, not a brony." She looks up at me. "Sorry, this isn't going to work."

Then she looks back down at her packet, takes out a pen, and starts to make notes on what I'm beginning to suspect is a *My Little Pony* questionnaire. She looks really into it, like it would be rude to interrupt her, and before I know it, there's a BONG.

Without taking her eyes off the paper, the girl slides down to her right, and a very petite blonde takes her place. She at least starts out by smiling at me.

"Hi," I say.

Her mouth opens and it looks like she's saying the word *hi* back, but I can't hear her for the life of me.

"Sorry, it's so loud in here." I raise my voice a little to be heard over the din. "I'm Graham."

Her mouth opens again and this time it looks like lots of words come out, but once again, I hear nothing.

"Sorry, could you repeat that?" I ask, leaning forward.

But I swear she must be on mute. Not a single syllable of her conversation gets over to me. I begin feeling self-conscious about the number of times I say "sorry," so at some point, I just start nodding. She beams at me. And when the sound of the gong comes, she slips something across the table to me before moving over. I look down. It's a piece of paper that says *Penny*, followed by her phone number.

"Sorry, I don't do gingers," a loud voice booms, and I look up to see a pretty but intimidating girl sporting a lip ring and staring at my hair.

"Um, okay . . . ," I start.

She stares at me. "But you do have really nice eyes. Could you take your glasses off?"

She is commanding, and I don't even think twice about doing exactly what she says. She leans over and blinks in my face.

"Really nice. What color would you say they are?"

"Um . . . blue?"

She tilts her head at me thoughtfully. "Sort of a stormy blue. Really unusual." She indicates for me to put the glasses back on. "I like those, too. Very Clark Kent/Superman."

I almost blush. The black-framed glasses are new and they sort of cost a fortune. But I replaced my wire-rimmed glasses for specifically that reason: because Roxana has a comic book crush on Clark Kent.

"Sorry, though. The ginger thing is still a deal breaker."

BONG.

A girl dressed like SpongeBob SquarePants sits across from me and proceeds to talk for the entire three minutes without asking me a single question.

BONG.

A tough-looking girl tells me she's a wrestler and won't date guys who are shorter than six-three or weigh less than 250.

BONG.

A pretty brunette with a nice smile introduces herself as Louisa and actually reaches over to shake my hand. But then she immediately looks apologetic.

"I'm sorry," she says.

"Let me guess, you don't do gingers either," I say, flicking at my hair.

She laughs. "No, that's not it. It's just . . . I'm in love with someone else."

Well, finally. Someone I have something in common with.

"He's over there at the purple table," she says, turning slightly in her chair to look. "I thought maybe this would make him jealous."

My own eyes flick over to the purple table, and I immediately pick out Roxana. A guy with dark hair sits across from her and she laughs at something he says. I scowl.

"Sorry. I know it's stupid!" Louisa says, thinking the scowl is for her.

I shake my head. "No, not stupid. In fact, I know exactly how you feel."

"Really?" She brightens. "Isn't it awful?"

"Kinda," I agree.

"And I guess kinda exhilarating," she says. "I mean, I've never been in love before."

"Me neither. But now I sorta understand pop songs. It's definitely weird."

"Yes!" Louisa declares. "Why is Z100 suddenly playing the soundtrack to my mind?"

"Whoa. Doubly cruel."

She smiles.

BONG.

She sighs. "Guess I made my bed with this one," she says as she slides down a seat and wishes me good luck before she turns unenthusiastically to her new partner.

"You too."

I notice something immediately about the girl who sits in front of me now. It's on her wrist, it's paper, it's silver, and it says ZINC on it.

I stare wide-eyed at her.

"Hi," she says. She's black, with a smattering of freckles on her nose, and her dark hair is in a thick braid over her shoulder. There's a bright red streak in it.

"Um . . . ," I start, before I realize I really have nothing left to lose. "Hi, I'm Graham. Is there anything I can do to get that wristband from you?" I point to it.

She bursts out laughing. "Sense of humor—check."

"I'm serious," I mutter.

"Okay, then never mind," she says. "Deranged—check." She stares at me. "I'll have you know I waited all night for this wristband."

"Me too," I say darkly.

"Ohhhh." Understanding dawns in her eyes. "Were you one of the ones who got screwed 'cause of the bum rush?"

I nod.

"Jackasses," she responds. "I was only able to keep my place because of my sharp elbows. One of the perks of being New York City born and bred." She taps one of her elbows like it's a Thoroughbred that just won a race for her. "That blows, though, I'm sorry."

I shrug.

"Maybe someone will post a video of the panel. There's a forum I go to that's pretty good for Zinc stuff if you're really into him. It's called z-men.net."

Despite myself, I smile. Weakly. "Yup, I'm on there."

She visibly brightens. "Oh, what's your screen name?"

"ScribePoz."

"Oh, hey, I know you!" she says, grinning now. "You wrote some prequel chapters about Charlie Noth, right? With him getting his first publishing deal?"

I'm startled. "Yeah, that's me." I've never met a stranger who's read my stuff before.

"That was good," she says, her gaze livelier now. "I really liked that you had the story within the story and went into what his book was about."

Whoa. And a stranger with compliments to boot.

"Thanks," I say.

She looks at her wristband. "Damn. Now I'm actually sorry I can't give this to you. Since I know you're a true fan and all."

I smile at her. "Thanks. For being sorry, I mean."

"I'm Amelia, by the way."

BONG.

"Well, I'm Earhart5921 on the forum," she says as she's getting up. "Maybe I'll see you around there?"

"Yeah, maybe." I smile at her.

The next girl is a curvy blonde, and so is the one right after her. They're twins. And their responses are almost as identical as they are. I feel like I have déjà vu when I speak to the second one.

BONG.

Short. Tall. Crazy-colored hair. Mousy-colored hair. Costumed. In a T-shirt. My head is spinning with the possibilities, and it doesn't really matter anyway, because none of them are Roxy.

Finally, thankfully, the girl with the clipboard gets back on the mic to let us know that our session is over.

I slowly gather up my backpack, deliberately not making eye contact with Penny, or Amelia, or any of the other girls I just spent three intense minutes with. By the time I get to the door of the conference room, Casey and Felicia are already there, and they're chatting animatedly. It's a weird sight because I'm not sure I've ever seen them hold a conversation with each other before.

"Hey!" Felicia says when she sees me approaching. "How did it go?"

I shrug and then I look at her hand, which is holding at least fifteen tiny slips of paper, the kind that was on the table for those who wanted to exchange information. "It went well for you, I see."

She shrugs. "There were some nice guys there. And some cute ones. But shall ever the twain meet? That is the question."

I'm not surprised. When you look like Felicia, you're dressed like Wonder Woman, and you're at New York Comic Con . . . there is only one logical result. I can only wonder what was wrong with the other five guys who didn't give her their number. Probably too intimidated.

I sneak a peek at Casey and am surprised to see that he has a few slips of papers in his hand also. "You got some too?" I say incredulously, before I realize how that sounds and immediately wish I could take it back.

Casey sighs and goes to put the slips away. "Some of the girls were cool," he grumbles, "and they seemed to like me."

"That's not what I meant, Case," I start. "That came out wrong. I'm sorry." And it's true. Casey is a great guy, but before this whole weird thing with Callie, he'd really never shown much interest in something as mundane as dating. I always thought there were too many unknown factors for him, too much he couldn't control.

He shrugs. "Well, I guess I gotta find some replacement for Callie," he retorts. "Now that that's off the table."

Ah! Maybe one tiny good thing did come from us not getting the Zinc wristbands: I will no longer have to figure that headache out.

"Hey, guys," a cheerful voice says behind me, and I prepare myself to turn around and see if Roxana has any telltale slips of paper.

But what I see is much, much worse.

She's grinning from ear to ear, and right behind her, following her like a tall, buff puppy dog, is some guy. Some guy with jet-black hair and bright blue eyes, wearing all black except for some outrageously colored Converses on his feet.

"This is Devin. It turns out he's going to the inking panel next too."

I continue to stare at his feet. I see. Those are illustrations on his Converses that he probably drew himself. He's an artist, just like Roxana.

And then Devin opens his mouth to say hello, and my heart sinks even further.

The asshole is freaking British.

Chapter 8
THE BRITISH INVASION

WE'RE SLOWLY INCHING OUR WAY FORWARD IN THE BOWELS OF THE JAVITS
Center, toward Room 1A04, where the inking panel is taking place.
Casey leaves us when we reach the stairs. He's scheduled himself to get
three artists to sign some books.

"I'll have exactly twenty-five minutes for lunch at one thirty," he says,
looking at his watch. "Not sure that's enough time for the food court."
He's probably right. We found out last year just how long the lines
could get at the food court.

"Hot dog stand at the top of the stairs?" I suggest.

He nods. "Meet you there?"

"One thirty. Got it."

He jets off and I'm left with Felicia, Roxy, and, of course, now Devin, who is currently going on and on about his "gap year" from "university." Kill me.

"I hopped around California and Arizona for a month or so, but I haven't been able to bring myself to leave New York yet. It's just too amazing."

"Isn't it the best?" Roxana gushes. "I'm hoping I can go to college in the city."

"Completely. Though, I admit, my money is running out faster here too," Devin says cheerfully, and I wonder if there's a wikiHow for hacking into a bank account, zeroing it out, and forcing the owner of it to cut his "gap year" short.

"Ah, here we are," he says as we reach the end of a line of people outside one of the closed beige doors that leads to the panel room.

"So this is a panel about drawing, right?" Felicia asks, and I see her consulting her schedule.

"Yup," Roxana says. "Well, inking specifically."

"I hope they don't only have digital artists," Devin says. "I still prefer to do mine with old-fashioned marker and paper."

"Me too!" Roxana answers a little too enthusiastically. *Geez, could she make it any more obvious,* I think moodily.

But Devin seems to have no problem with the blatant flirtation, matching Roxy's excited tone with a British-tinged one of his own. Of course. Obviously the idiot has exquisite taste in women.

I watch them flirt on line for as long as I can stand (and amuse myself with a quick aside about them flirting on line as opposed to *online*, the traditional method of modern flirting), and am luckily distracted by Felicia precisely at the moment I think I've hit maximum anxiety levels.

"Oooh! Gary Chatham is going to be on Stage One-D at four p.m." She looks up at me. "Could I get into that?"

I look at her schedule. Gary Chatham is a big star promoting a big new blockbuster, so I have a feeling it's in one of the main hall panels. Which means she might have to try to get a wristband for it, and it's likely those are already gone at this point.

The schedule tells me my assumption is correct. "You have to line up for a wristband, near the front entrance," I tell her. "You might want to go and try now, but it's possible they're all gone already."

"Oh, really?" she asks. "Hmmmm . . ."

I can see her trying to determine whether or not to leave us to give it a go, but she ultimately shrugs. "I don't want to go by myself, I think. You guys have other plans at four, right?"

Ugh! I was supposed to have other plans. I was supposed to be coming out of the Zinc panel and sweeping Roxana off her feet. But now . . .

No, seriously, I can't give up. Maybe I can go over to the room where the Zinc panel is and see if there's any possible way to get in. Maybe there's a weak point in the guarding or ticket-checking systems. I admit, I'm better at brainstorming fantasy-adventure scenarios than, say, heist movies, but this is for true love, and that's a goal that binds together every genre on the planet.

Of course, going to investigate the Zinc situation might mean leaving Roxana and Devin alone together.

"By the way, I didn't tell you, but that is an excellent Pris costume," he's now saying to her.

She laughs. "Thanks, but . . ." She points to her green ear. *That's right, idiot. The costume is not from* Blade Runner, I think triumphantly.

Devin only looks confused, which makes me think . . . "Did she have a green ear in the movie?" he asks, puzzled. Whoa! Does he really not know who Althena is?

"*The Chronicles of Althena*?" Roxana asks. "You do know what that is? Right?"

"Um . . . ," Devin starts, and I am immediately gloating. "You know, I think I've vaguely heard of it." Yes! Yes! Yes! He's got to be getting so many deductions right now.

But instead of frowning at him, Roxana is smiling mischievously. "Vaguely heard of it? Oh, man, that is so sad for you."

Devin merely grins back. "Then enlighten me, not-Pris."

What the hell? How does he turn his utter and offensive lack of knowledge of one of Roxana's favorite things into more flirting?

Roxana bows. "*The Chronicles of Althena*," she rattles off, "was an American comic series that ran for two years from 1991 through 1993, by the incomparable writer and artist Robert Zinc. It was published by the then newly established Young Guns Press. And it was—is—utterly brilliant."

Devin's bright blue eyes flash even brighter. "Tell me more," he says. "What is it about?"

"Well . . . I can give you a *brief* synopsis. But you're definitely going to have to read it for yourself," Roxana says, crossing her arms.

"All right," Devin says. "I defer to your expertise on that."

"But basically it's about an alien, Althena, who crash-lands on Earth to do a research project and meets a failed sci-fi writer named Charlie Noth. Althena's knowledge of humankind is pretty limited, though, and comes mostly from an outdated sci-fi movie marathon her lazy Homo Sapiens Studies instructor fed her in school. Hence . . ." She swoops her arm up to indicate herself.

"Ah, of course. I see. Hence *Blade Runner* . . ." Devin glances over at me and grins like he's just discovered the theory of relativity. "And Mad Max!" He taps at his ear to indicate he has now noticed that I also have a green ear. Needless to say, I'm not impressed.

"Right!" Roxana says as if she is. "And here's a fun fact: Zinc based the character of Noth on himself. He started out as a sci-fi author, you see, and not a very successful one. He was feeling really jaded about that industry when he started writing *Althena*. Anyway, read the original series. They are wonderful. Zinc has these gorgeous panels, coupled with just the perfect words, and it's just like poetry, really. Comic book poetry."

I'm starting to smile despite myself because hearing Roxana talk so reverently about something I also deeply love is intoxicating.

"The original?" Devin asks. "As opposed to . . ."

"Oh. Right. So Zinc and Young Guns had a huge falling-out. That's why the series only ran for two years. Afterward Zinc basically disappeared. But Young Guns owned the rights to Althena. There wasn't any overt interest for a long time, but pretty soon the fansites started to get traction and some of the kids who were fans when they were teens started to get old enough to become, like, executives. So long story short, five years ago, there was a reboot." She pauses dramatically.

"And . . . we do not like this reboot?" Devin asks.

"No, sir, we do not," Roxana says emphatically. "It has none of the subtlety or the nuance. And certainly none of that otherworldly art."

"Or the humor." I can't help but butt in now. "No sly little jokes."

Roxana looks at me and snorts. "Those guys don't know no Sly that isn't a Stallone."

"Idiots!" I proclaim.

"Fools!" she responds, not missing a beat.

"So then . . . you guys think the movie is going to suck too?" Felicia interrupts our well-rehearsed dialogue. "I thought you were excited for that panel today."

"Ah, well, we *did* think the movie was going to suck," Roxana starts, and then turns to me to continue.

I oblige. "But then word got out that Zinc himself—who hasn't been heard from in twenty years, mind you—that he had actually given the film his stamp of approval."

"Which means that the movie has to be based on the original," Roxana concludes. "And Zinc being here today basically confirms that." She looks at me, and I can see all the excitement and disappointment pooled together in her eyes.

"It does," I say as my mind goes into overdrive. I should treat this panel problem like brainstorming one of our stories. That's how I'll figure it out, by thinking *What would Lockbreak do?*

"Ah, right," Devin cuts in again with his perfect British accent. "I had been hearing mutterings about him. So, really, no one's heard from him in twenty years?"

"Not a peep." Roxana turns to him. "No photographs. No interviews. No social media. There were even rumors that he was dead."

The doors to the room we're standing by finally open and a stream of people file out as Roxana continues to tell Devin some of the more outrageous theories surrounding Zinc over the years: That he was an alien himself. That he never existed. That he has spent the past decade running a tantric yoga retreat in East Chatham, New York.

We're finally let inside. They don't clear out these smaller rooms between panels, so there are quite a few people already seated by the time we get in, likely taking in a block of panels at once. We find two seats in one row and two a row behind it. Without consulting anyone, Devin walks in after Roxana as she slides into the row closer to the stage. I scowl as Felicia and I are forced to sit behind them.

"Hi, and welcome to Inking Techniques, everyone," the panel moderator says from the stage, then begins to introduce the panelists.

I'm forced to watch as Devin leans way too close to Roxana's ear to whisper something to her, and as she laughs at whatever he says. Really? Like, how funny can he possibly be about the moderator's introduction? Also, he should shut up since the panel has started now.

I force myself to take deep breaths.

Get it together, Posner, I think. *Focus on getting Roxana into the Zinc panel and it won't matter what sweet nothings Devin whispers into her ear.*

Because, above all, Roxy is a Z-man.

"I think I might be getting the hang of the communication intricacies of Homo sapiens," Althena says in Issue #4. **"You never say what you mean. Your brain must function as a highly evolved translation program factoring in posture, eye movement, vocal tone, context of dialogue . . . otherwise no one would ever comprehend anyone else."**

"I'm not sure anyone does comprehend anyone else," Charlie replies while a thought bubble expresses his true feelings. **"And the only one who seems to understand my every feeling is not even human."**

It's true—we never say what we mean. But for once, I want to. And I want to say it to the one person who understands *me* better than anyone.

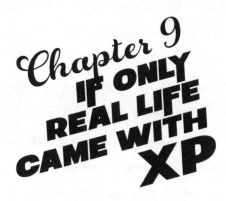

Chapter 9
IF ONLY REAL LIFE CAME WITH XP

AFTER THE INKING PANEL, I MAKE MY DECISION AND (PAINFULLY) LEAVE
Roxana and Devin to their own devices. I tell them I'll meet them at
the hot dog stand with Casey at one thirty.

That gives me thirty minutes to root out what I can about the Zinc
panel, which is hopefully enough time to gather some useful intel about
getting us in. But hopefully *not* enough time for Roxana and the British
stud muffin (crumpet?) to fall irrevocably in love.

I make my way over to where the Zinc panel will be, Stage 1-E,
which is the smaller of one of the two main halls. These halls are
reserved for only a few special events, and the Zinc panel at 3 p.m.

is only 1-E's second of the day, followed by an advance screening of *Godzilla: Unleashed* at 6 p.m. Just as I told Felicia earlier, everything here needs wristbands. ROOMS WILL BE CLEARED OUT BETWEEN EACH PANEL IN THE MAIN HALLS AND WRISTBANDS WILL BE CHECKED, a sign tells me in the con's signature Comic Sans font (which, besides actual comic books, is the only place Comic Sans is ever called for). ABSOLUTELY NO PHOTOGRAPHY OR VIDEOGRAPHY. ANYONE CAUGHT FILMING OR TAKING PICTURES WILL IMMEDIATELY BE ESCORTED OUT OF THE ROOM, another sign reads, adding insult to injury.

There are people lined up in front of 1-E already, every one of them adorned with a silver-colored piece of paper around their wrist. I've never been so jealous of a piece of sticky paper in my life. And then, worst of all, I catch a glimpse of the Zinc hater in the Papa Smurf hat. Unbelievable. *He* gets to see Robert Zinc and Roxana and I don't?

There's a curly-haired guy in a teal Comic Con staff shirt standing guard in front of the line. I try to exhale my anger out before I approach him.

"Excuse me," I say, putting on an I-promise-I-am-polite-and-rational smile and asking him something I'm sure he's heard at least a dozen times today, "but is there any way I can get into this panel?"

"Do you have a wristband?" he asks, not in an unfriendly tone.

"No," I say. He starts to shake his head, but I continue, "I actually waited in line for it since last night. I was number one hundred and three in line, so I should've had one. But then there was a great big bum rush and all these people cut ahead of me." I realize exactly what I'm doing: the nerd whine. But nothing is beneath me at this point. If he asked me to grovel, or lick the floor, or sing an Ariana Grande ballad in front of the whole con, I would do it. "It's just . . . really unfair." And my nerdgradation is complete.

To his credit, the guy is not a jerk about it. In fact, he seems to listen pretty sympathetically and when he tells me he's sorry and he understands, he actually seems to mean it. "I really wish there was something I could do, but I honestly can't. Even *I* can't get into this panel," he says.

Time to level up. "May I speak to a supervisor?" I ask. I can almost feel the glare of the dozens of Z-men (and that imposter) on line boring through the back of my head right now. I want to tell them that I'm not normally this guy. I'm not the guy at the restaurant who sends food back to the kitchen, or the person who's rude to the customer service guy on the phone, or the asswipe who posts spoilers on threads without the appropriate warnings. But today . . . today, I have to be. I have to go against my nice-guy, keep-the-peace, avoid-confrontation grain and be confident and forceful. Like a more manly avatar of myself. For Roxy's sake.

The curly-haired guy gets on his walkie-talkie, and a couple of minutes later, another staffer with a shaved head and some gauges in his ear approaches us. He doesn't really look older or more in charge than the curly-haired guy, but his voice does have somewhat more of an edge of authority about it.

I explain my situation again, and he lets me finish before shaking his head. "I completely understand your frustration, but there is literally nothing we can do. We've already spoken to the film studio sponsoring the panel about the situation. I can tell you that they're trying to come up with a make-good. But as of now, unless you have one of those wristbands with a bar code on it, you can't even get down this hallway anymore." He looks over at the small line of people already there and frowns. "Actually, none of these people are even supposed to be here until two thirty."

Yikes. I know some of the people in line have been listening to this whole ordeal, and I can feel them shifting around. If they get kicked out of their primo positions because of me, I'll be a marked man. Not that I'd personally feel bad if Papa Smurf or any of the other bum rush douches lost out on the privilege, but my fight-or-flight instincts are also reminding me of my less-than-buff physique.

"Thanks for your help anyway," I mumble before skedaddling out of the hallway and leaving the two staffers to do what they will.

I mope all the way to the hot dog stand as capes of all colors swish past me. I almost get my eyes gouged out by a selfie stick being flailed around by a guy running after an almost-seven-foot-tall Darth Vader, shouting "Lord Vader!" He finally gets Vader's attention and snaps the all-important photo with him. Someone stops me to ask if they can take a photo of my costume too. I'm glad I can keep my face in brood mode as they do. After all, it goes with the costume.

(I don't think hunky eighties action stars were contractually allowed to smile.)

I make it to the hot dog stand around 1:15 p.m. and spend the next ten minutes still trying to come up with a way to make the panel happen, hoping someone's costume will inspire me. Unfortunately, death rays and samurai swords are useless for problem-solving in the real world, even at Comic Con.

When Casey approaches me, his face looks about as thunderous as I feel.

"Look. At. This," he says through gritted teeth. He holds up his copy of *The Walking Dead* #1 and shows me an enormous silver streak that is now spread out across Officer Rick Grimes's ass.

"What happened?"

"I waited in line for an hour and three minutes. One hour and three," he says. "The guy in front of me had a rolling suitcase and he had forty-seven individual covers signed. I counted. And then, *then* . . ." He takes in a deep breath. "Robert Kirkman signs mine and an assistant next to him takes it from him and hands it to me. And I step away to look at it and . . ." He's holding the issue so hard as he thrusts it in front of my face that I'm pretty sure he's doing his own damage to it, a sure sign that he's legitimately shaken up. "I mean, if I ever need to ID the moron . . ."

Upon closer inspection, I can see that the silver streak is actually a perfect thumbprint. "Wow," I say. "You didn't say anything?"

"Oh, I tried to get back on the line. But Kirkman's time slot was already running over and they couldn't 'accommodate' me. Did I mention rolling suitcase guy? And his *forty-seven* comics? I bet each and every one of them has a freaking perfect autograph on it."

"Oh, man. I'm sorry, Case," I say, shaking my head.

"I didn't even make any of my other signings." He looks around the convention floor morosely. "That's an excellent Howard the Duck," he mutters as he points out a costume.

I look over. He's right. The white feathers, bill, and leather jacket were put together with extra care. I give the guy a nod of appreciation. Howard the Duck was one of the movies I inherited from my mom's extensive collection, which was heavily centered on films of the 1980s, and one of the few that Casey seems to like more than Roxana does. Though we've all picked up a few of the original comic books since and appreciated it for its irreverent, oddball humor.

Casey lets out a final sigh, and then I can actually see him regrouping his emotions to focus on the next task at hand. "Where's everyone else? I'm pretty hungry," he asks.

"They should be coming. I left them to go check out the Zinc panel situation. See if there was any way in."

"And?" he asks, but he doesn't seem terribly surprised when I shake my head. "I think it was pretty obvious this morning that we weren't getting in," he says in a slightly obnoxious matter-of-fact tone. "You have to let it go, Graham." Easy for him to say. Sure, Casey gets upset and angry just like everyone else, but his ability to quickly reassess the situation and then move on is slightly inhuman. And, I should add, a little indecent.

"Let what go?" I hear Roxy's voice and turn around to see her, Devin, and Felicia approaching us.

"Oh, the Zinc panel," Casey answers. "Graham went to see if he could get in."

"Oh, is that where you ran off to?" Roxana looks at me.

"Yeah," I mutter, feeling kind of pissy toward Casey. I didn't exactly want to bring it up to Roxana again unless I had miraculously done the impossible and could be suitably revered for it.

"Yeah, but no dice." Casey continues his winning streak. "It's impossible."

Roxana sighs. "Figured as much."

Thanks a lot, dude, I think as I glare at my friend. Probably unfairly, but it doesn't matter too much because he doesn't notice. Picking up on social cues has never been Casey's strong suit.

"Well, look, we shouldn't mope around while the panel comes and goes, right?" Devin says, and I immediately reposition the direction of my glare. "How about we do something so spectacularly fun that we all forget we're missing Mr. Elusive Comic Book Writer?"

He asks Felicia if he can look at the schedule she's holding, and she hands it over. But I notice that even Roxana is looking at him incredulously, and I can't help but be a little pleased. Maybe she'll tire of this jerk soon and we can finally lose him.

"Aha!" Devin says as he looks up triumphantly from the booklet. "I've found the perfect thing." He looks Roxana, Felicia, and then *me* up and down and grins.

"Not more speed dating, is it?" I ask.

"Nope. It's a costume contest. Starting at two thirty. And I think you, Felicia, and Roxana should enter."

Chapter 10
DRESSED FOR SUCCESS

WE WOLF DOWN SOME HOT DOGS AND PRETZELS, AND THEN CASEY EASILY AND wisely begs off the costume contest, since he has a stringent schedule to adhere to. I consider going off with him. But then I see that Roxana and Felicia seem game to get whisked off by Devin and I decide not to risk leaving them alone again.

So I reluctantly acquiesce. I like my costume, but I know full well it's not creative enough to win anything. Anyway, that wasn't the point when I came up with it (the point was to impress Roxana . . . obviously). There's no way Felicia is going to win anything as one of the dozens of Wonder Women here. I glance over at Roxana and the perfect bandit's mask she's painted over her eyes. *Maybe she has a chance,* I think. But the truth is, people can get pretty elaborate here.

Case in point: we get stuck behind someone who's wearing giant eight-foot-tall wings and is having a pretty hard time maneuvering through the crowds. As we follow him at a snail's pace, it eventually becomes clear that he's headed to the same room we are.

It's one of the bigger conference rooms, similar in size to the speed dating one. But this one is filled with seemingly every instance of spandex, feather, glitter, cardboard, chrome, and sequin that the con has. It's hard to know where to look.

A Dalek and a few Doctors (two twelfths, one tenth, and one fourth) are to my right. I count at least two almost complete sets of X-Men. Stormtroopers and Reys stand guard throughout the room. Dozens of soldiers wearing white pants and tall, strappy boots herald the *Attack on Titan* congregation. Wildly colored wigs assure that the rest of the manga crowd is appropriately represented. A headless horseman towers at least two feet above everybody in the room. It's pure madness.

"Graham! Look who the judges are," Roxana says, and I turn to where she's pointing. I see some reality star that I think is a Real Housekeeper or something, and then an obnoxious stand-up comedian I don't much care for. I'm confused until the Housewife sits down and her voluminous hair reveals the small, bearded guy behind her.

"Emmett Shah!" I grin. He's one of my favorite writers, and I hadn't realized he was going to be here.

"Oh, excuse me! I need to get my friends on there." Devin is motioning to a staffer who's walking around with a clipboard, getting everyone who wants to participate in the contest to sign up.

"Sure thing." The staffer smiles at him as she hands the clipboard over. Devin asks both Felicia and Roxana to spell their last names before turning to me. "And your last name?"

I look down at my clothing. "It's okay. I really don't think my costume is good enough for this."

"Sure it is," Devin says at the same time that Roxana chimes in with, "Of course it is." They look at each other and grin like coconspirators. Great.

"His last name is Posner. *P-o-s-n-e-r*," Roxana supplies to Devin, who fills it in.

"All of you need to show off your work," Devin says as he nods.

"Definitely. And you can meet Emmett Shah, Graham!" Roxana exclaims. The girl does speak the truth.

Well, the one good thing to come out of this is that we soon get separated from uncostumed Devin as we're whisked into lines for each of our categories. Felicia gets sent to the Superheroes line, while Roxana and I end up in the Sci-Fi line. There are also lines for Anime/Manga, Fantasy, Video Games, and a catch-all Miscellaneous line, where I see that the winged creature we were originally following has ended up.

As I get in line next to her, I can't help but be reminded of the years Roxy and I spent trick-or-treating together. Our costumes ranged from the store-bought and sort of lazy (there were definitely Hogwarts robes for at least a couple of years) to obscure sources of pride. In seventh grade, the last year we took to the streets to score some candy, we dressed as Charlie and Althena—though with less attention to detail than we've paid today. It was the year we both discovered Zinc. No one except for Casey really figured out who were supposed to be, but we didn't care. We were totally smitten with our new obsession, and we spent more time trying to remember lines of dialogue from Charlie and Althena's Halloween meeting than knocking on doors.

"Uncanny," Charlie keeps saying as he stares and stares at Althena's Pris costume.

"Does that word mean something different every time you say it?" Althena asks, genuinely curious about how human language works.

But Charlie assumes she's just teasing him. **"Sorry,"** he replies. **"It's just . . . are you sure you're not actually Daryl Hannah?"**

And now Roxana stands beside me again, dressed specifically as Althena-as-Pris, and I know, in a way that twelve-year-old me could never have imagined, exactly how Charlie felt: a whirlpool of unbidden emotions, of excitement and fear and novelty churning just beneath the surface of my skin. Only, instead of meeting someone new, it's been like having a switch turned on, shedding light on something—and someone—that's actually been there the whole time but is just now being revealed for all that it is.

At the front of our line, a short girl with a cloud of curly hair, wearing an NYCC staff T-shirt, explains the rules of the costume contest in a mumbled monotone. "You will go up in groups of ten and you will each stand in front of the judges for ten seconds. At this point, feel free to strike whatever poses you feel show your costumes to best advantage," she says . . . I think. It's not super easy to hear her above the din of six other staffers giving the same speech. Especially since her hair seems to catch most of her consonants.

Then I hear something about being rated, something about adding up scores . . . mumble, mumble, mumble . . . "and that's how we announce the winner!" She says this last part in the loudest and most enthusiastic tone I've heard from her yet. Probably because her speech is over.

"What?" I ask Roxana.

"I seriously have no idea," Roxana replies. "I think I caught four words of that."

A guy in front of us who's dressed in a lovingly made Predator costume helpfully chimes in. "She said we go up in groups of ten, then get rated from one to ten in each group by each judge. The numbers get added up, and the top three from each group make it to the next round. It goes on like that until there's only one winner from each group, and then those group winners go into the finals. But there are prizes for winning your group as well as the final."

"Wow," I say as I stare up at his imposing figure, unable to tell if he's on stilts or really just that tall. "You heard all that through your mask?"

He lightly taps his steel-gray face covering, which actually does sound like it's made of metal, and shrugs. "I've worn this thing so much, I think it's heightened my senses."

"Apropos," I say, thinking of the technologically evolved alien he's portraying.

"Indeed," he agrees. "Ah, I thought you were Mad Max for a second," he adds. "But now I see the ear. Oh, both of you. Good ones." He indicates Roxy.

I nod and smile. It's usually good to meet fellow Althenians. You know, when they're not cutting in front of you in a highly important line and destroying your life in the process.

We're getting herded onstage now, and Predator turns back around to see where he's walking.

"Let's do this!" Roxana says before putting up her hand for a high five. I give her one.

Our group of ten gets evenly dispersed onstage and told again that we can do whatever poses we like. Predator lifts his claws and roars. He definitely has practiced that before. I kind of just stand there. Althena doesn't really have any poses, per se. But then I see what Roxana is doing and I laugh.

She's aerobicizing—what Althena's subpar Homo Sapiens Studies class assured her all humans do for both recreation and exercise. She's alternating between performing high knee kicks and throwing her hands out rhythmically.

"Come on, Graham!" she yells.

God help me, I cannot resist anything this girl asks of me. And so I fall into rhythm beside her, following her moves like she's Richard Simmons and I'm the Prancercise lady trapped in a gangly teenager's body.

"Thank you! Please step off the stage and we'll notify the three of you who made it to the next round," a staffer on a microphone says.

"I can't believe you made me aerobicize in front of Emmett Shah!" I try to chide Roxy, but I know she can hear the laughter in my voice.

"You cannot half-ass a Comic Con costume contest," she responds.

"One, two . . ." An NYCC staffer pulls us out of the line and then goes down a few people to get someone in a very elaborate half-HAL, half-Dave costume (astronaut helmet and a wide-eyed stare from the front, and a sinister-looking large red dot attached to the back of his head). "Three," the staffer said. "You guys have made it to the next round. Please go line up on that side of the room."

Predator congratulates us before sauntering off with the rest of our line.

"Wow, really?" I'm kind of stunned as I walk over with our *2001* companion.

"Why are you surprised?" Roxana asks. "We look pretty amazing." She winks at me.

I look over and see that Felicia is also miraculously standing over by the wall of winners from her group. I can't help but shake my head.

Even a Comic Con costume contest can become a beauty pageant in the end.

We go through the whole process again, and I actually make it to round three before I'm eliminated. Roxana goes on to the next round. I find Felicia on the reject side and she tells me she only made it to round two.

We cheer as Roxana continues to *Flashdance*-jog her way into the judges' hearts. She gets eliminated in the fifth round, one to go before the final.

"You were robbed!" I yell when she walks over to us.

She shrugs good-naturedly. "I can't beat that guy's HAL impression. I'm not entirely sure that's not the actual guy who plays him in there!"

I consider the costume again. The kid's face behind the astronaut helmet doesn't look any older than twenty. "If HAL has found the Sorcerer's Stone."

"A robot with the power of eternal youth?" Roxana asks. "Seems kind of redundant."

I shake my head. "A robot with the power to dangle eternal youth in front of the lowly humans he seeks to control."

"Ah!" she says, and nods. "Got it. Terrifying."

As it turns out, HAL/Dave is not the final winner from our group either. That honor goes to someone dressed as *Serenity*, the ship from *Firefly*, complete with a working gangway.

In the final group are a really detailed Groot; a character with elaborate purple hair I don't recognize; *Serenity*; two people dressed together
as the Batman Slap meme; a White Walker; and someone in a high-
necked, old-fashioned dress, with a covered wagon over her head, and
carrying a sign that says I HAVE DYSENTERY à la this old-school computer game called *Oregon Trail*. The last rightfully ends up taking the
grand prize, and the entire room breaks out into loud applause as the
girl picks up her $200 gift card for Forbidden Planet.

"Come on," Roxana says to me, and before I know it, she has slipped
her hand into mine and locked arms with Felicia on her other side and
is expertly guiding us back to the front of the room.

"Where are we going?" I ask, but I don't get a response until we stop.

"Excuse me, Mr. Shah," she politely says to the balding head in front
of us that is still facing the stage. The writer turns around. "Sorry to
bother you. We're just huge fans. My friend Graham especially. He's a
brilliant writer too."

She indicates me, and I blush furiously as Emmett puts out his hand
to shake mine.

"An aspiring writer." I correct Roxy's assessment of me as I let go of
her hand to pump his.

Emmett grins. "Do you write a lot?" he asks.

I nod. "Try to. We have sessions at least once a week." I turn to gesture to Roxana, who I notice is slipping away.

"Well, then. There's no aspiring about it. If you write, you're a writer.

Maybe getting paid for it is a different can of worms, but being a writer itself? Don't doubt that's what you are."

A slow smile spreads across my face. "Thank you, sir. That means a lot coming from you. I've read your work since I was little. All of it."

"Well, then, thank *you*. Graham, right?"

I nod.

"Good luck, Graham. And great costume." He gives me one last smile before taking a worn baseball cap from his back pocket, jamming it onto his head, and moving along toward the exit.

The smile on my face stays there as I watch him pick his way through the crowd. Wow. I just had a conversation with Emmett Shah and he made me feel like a real writer. I feel a little bit like I could fly.

I look for Roxy to thank her for making that happen. But when I finally find her, my mood instantly plummets.

She and Felicia are against the wall, talking again to Devin, who actually smiles when he sees me. "Hey, man! Did you have a good time?" he asks.

"Sure," I say. Christ. Does the stud crumpet have to be devastatingly handsome, British, and *nice*?

"So Devin just had a great idea," Roxana says. Oh, right. Let's not forget *brilliant*, too. Why not? "Devin?"

"Well, it's almost four p.m. and that Robert Zinc panel should be letting out. I thought maybe we could go stand near that hallway. Just in case he leaves that way? You guys wouldn't mind catching a glimpse of him, right?" He bestows a grin on all of us and I grouchily wonder what happened to the cliché that all Brits have terrible teeth.

Yeah, fine. It *is* a great idea.

Score a million points for you, Stud Crumpet, I think as I follow the three of them toward Stage 1-E, the scene of my most recent utter failure.

Chapter 11
CONFESSIONS OF A SECONDARY CHARACTER

THE STAFFERS FROM EARLIER WERE RIGHT—WE'RE NO LONGER ALLOWED TO GET anywhere near Stage 1-E. Ropes are set up right by the entrance to its hallway, guarded by staffers with scan guns. Right now, they mainly seem to be scanning green wristbands. I eye the reptilian silhouette on one of them and assume it's for the *Godzilla: Unleashed* screening.

I've texted Casey to let him know where we are, and he's approaching us now, holding something white and in a clear plastic casing above his head. "Got it," he says as he nears, flipping over his acquisition so that we can see it. "Peter Mayhew."

"Oh. Right." I look at the scrawled signature on my dad's picture and feel a little guilty for totally forgetting about that. But at least one Posner geek will be happy today.

"Did you try to get him to spill secrets about the upcoming films?" Devin asks.

I think he's joking, but Casey merely nods. "Yes, and I think I chose my question wisely."

"What was it?" I ask.

Casey looks me square in the eye and says, "'Mr. Mayhew, could you tell me what title you invoiced for?'"

We all give him a blank stare.

"What does that mean?" Roxana finally pronounces our collective confusion.

Casey blinks. "I thought he'd tell us the title of the new movie. You know, the one that his agent had to use for invoicing. Or at least the red herring title. I could have used that to try and scour some stuff out."

"Oh . . . ," Roxy says, valiantly keeping a straight face.

"I figured if I asked him out of the blue, he wouldn't have time to come up with a lie and he might answer. Like a reflex."

"And did he?" I ask.

Casey shakes his head. "He didn't seem to understand the question."

"Weird," Felicia says, not as successful at hiding her grin.

"Oh, Graham! Look!" Roxana taps my arm and points down the hallway.

I see them, coming toward me like a group of Inferi. Except, instead of ravenous and scary, they look dazed but elated. Their silver wrist-bands hang off their wrists, gleaming like unicorn blood. Their eyes have a radiant, glassy sheen, like they have just beheld a dazzling god.

As they get closer to us, I hear a soft buzz. Some of them are chattering.

"Wasn't he just . . . brilliant?"

"Oh my God. What he said about Noth's anger. And his loss."

But most of them are quietly reverent. Shoulders back and heads held high, like they're coming from a medieval royal court. A few look over at my costume and Roxana's and smile beatifically at us. There's even a guy who's got on the same Mad Max iteration of Althena I'm wearing. He gives me an excited nod.

I can barely muster the energy to move my head in return. I mostly want to punch all these people in the face. Which is weird for me. I don't usually have violent thoughts unless they're about fictional characters.

"Shall we ask them how it was?" Devin asks in a shockingly cheerful voice.

"No," I spit out bitterly and automatically. For once, I don't want to know the details of something I missed out on. I don't want to pore over fansites and message boards and get the scoop. I can't abide the secondhand reports this time, not when I was so close to seeing the real thing for myself.

And maybe that way, I can pretend it never happened.

Roxana looks over at me and I can see that she understands, that she feels it too. "Maybe it's better if we imagine what it was like instead," she says to Devin. "Hey." She turns to me again. "Maybe we can make an issue out of it? Like the Grand Mage is doing a tour and MH 237 gets chosen to host . . . but somehow the Misfits miss it." She smiles at me.

I try to smile back, but even for Roxana, I can barely muster it. "Maybe," I say.

"The Misfits?" Devin asks. "Like the band?"

"No, the Misfits of Mage High. It's the series Graham and I work on together," Roxana explains.

"It's really good," Felicia chimes in.

Roxana beams at her. "Thanks, Felicia."

Felicia shrugs. "Just telling the truth."

"Well, go on, then. Don't leave a bloke hanging. What's it about?" Devin asks.

"Well, as you might have guessed, a high school. Of mages."

"I had somehow deduced that much, yes."

"And then there are . . ."

"Let me guess. These misfits?"

"Correct. Wow, nothing gets by you," Roxana says.

Devin grins at her. "And wherefore are they misfits?"

"Well, most everyone at the school has a basic level of magical abilities. And they are able to control their powers well. But the Misfits have a concentrated amount of certain abilities. So they are superpowerful in some ways but weak in others. Eventually, they decide to band together. Try their hand at being superheroes instead of awkward, outcast teenagers."

"As you do." Devin is nodding. "I like it. I'd love to read some, if you wouldn't mind sharing."

Roxana grins shyly. "Sure, as long as it's okay with Graham." She glances over at me and I shrug helplessly. What can I possibly say that would make me come out looking like the good guy here? Certainly not *No you can't see our precious work and use it to woo the girl of my dreams so fuck off.*

Roxy turns back to Devin. "What about you? What sort of things do you draw?"

"Oh, I'm sort of working on a graphic novel. It's loosely based on my travels. You know, A Limey's Guide to Yanks sort of thing." Wonderful. So he writes and draws. "But as for drawing, I feel my influences lie in the Sergio Aragonés, Roz Chast realm . . . maybe a little Chris Ware thrown in."

"Wow. Sounds awesome." Roxy's eyes are shining. I can practically see balloon hearts in their reflections.

Suddenly, I realize how dismal things are looking. Today was supposed to be the most amazing day of my life. The day that I seized the bull by the horns and found the courage to do something spectacular. Maybe the day that I finally emerged with a girlfriend. Now here I am, watching a romantic comedy play out in front of me. And I'm the supporting character; the comic-relief best friend; the male Judy Greer.

There's a reason you don't ever see a movie from the point of view of that character. It would be abject misery.

"Oh, hi! Graham, right?"

I'm brought out of my dark thoughts by someone standing in front of me, smiling. It's Amelia, the Z-men girl from the speed dating thing. She's grinning from ear to ear.

"Listen, I'm running late for a panel, but I have something for you." She touches me lightly on the arm. "I'll send it through the message boards. So keep an eye out for it, okay?"

"Okay," I respond in a daze.

She grins at me mischievously before being swept away by the tide of people heading in her direction.

"Who was that?" Felicia asks.

"Oh. Someone I met at the thing."

"The thing?"

"You know. The speed dating thing."

She breaks out into a giant grin. "See! I told you it was a great idea."

I don't say anything, but I do suddenly think to look over at Roxana. I have this fleeting thought that maybe, just maybe, she will have seen that exchange—and she'll be jealous.

But she's not looking at me all. She's still caught up in conversation with double-oh-seven.

So, no, Felicia. It was a fucking terrible idea.

To add insult to injury, the last people trickle out of the Zinc panel and, of course, Robert Zinc—or what I imagine the twenty-years-aged version of him based on his last known photograph to be—is not one of them.

Our one chance to see him is gone for good.

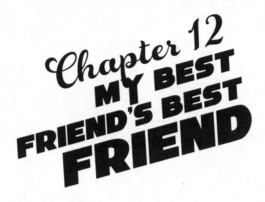

Chapter 12
MY BEST FRIEND'S BEST FRIEND

IN OUR LAST HOUR AT COMIC CON, CASEY DISAPPEARS TO TEND TO HIS SCHEDULE
again while Roxana picks up her sketchbook from Lacey Grotowski.
We all ooh and aah at the playful rendering of Althena Lacey created.

Then we spend some time browsing an actual comics booth. I'm flipping through a box when I hear Devin's accent cut through with, "Oh,
check this out, Roxana. This is one of my favorite covers of all time."

I look up to see him reach for an old Flash comic that's hanging in
plastic from a clothesline set up in front of the booth.

"May I help you?" A cold voice rings out. The guy manning the booth
has shot his arm out with such force, to stop Devin from touching his

comic, that it has sent the entire line swinging. The plastic-covered books crackle like a flock of disturbed crows.

"Oh, sorry." Devin grins. "I just wanted to show my friend that cover. . . ."

"And is she unable to see it from where she stands? Did she forget her glasses?"

"Uh . . ."

I'm not ashamed to admit that it does feel a little bit delightful to see Devin rendered speechless.

"Normally," the guy continues, dull gray eyes boring down at Devin, "one does not just reach out and touch a piece of merchandise that clearly has a six-hundred-dollar price tag on it." He's standing in front of the clothesline in a wide stance, with his hands on his hips; I'm sure he has no idea he is mimicking the very cover whose honor he seems so keen to defend.

"Right. Very sorry," Devin says, looking sheepish and backing away from the stand with his arms up.

I probably shouldn't be enjoying how much of a dick that guy is being, but . . .

"Geez. What a douche nozzle," Roxana says as she follows Devin out of the booth. "He just totally Gollumed you. 'My precioussssss.'" She hunches over and speaks in a spot-on Andy Serkis imitation.

Devin laughs.

And . . . enjoyment over.

The two of them bond shamelessly over the encounter for a seemingly endless stretch of booths until Felicia pipes up with, "Ooh, guys. Let's do this."

This turns out to be a photo booth that Geico is sponsoring. She somehow gets all four of us to cram into it so that small parts of our chins, cheeks, and foreheads can be captured for posterity pressed up against a CGI lizard.

At the end, she hands me one of the photos as a keepsake. Devin's chiseled features are front and center, right next to Roxy's beaming face. All you see of me is my right eye shooting daggers in Devin's direction. Wonderful.

I've now cycled through exactly three intense emotions. First, devastation at everything that has gone so spectacularly wrong. Then, anger at everything that has gone so spectacularly wrong, with an irrational level of venom directed toward Stud Crumpet. And finally, after an appropriate amount of stewing, that anger seems to have generated something a lot more useful: determination.

There are loads of things happening over the next couple of days at NYCC, including—as luck would have it—this amazing John Hughes panel that I've managed to keep a secret from Roxy, having begged her not to look at Saturday's schedule so that I could make it a surprise. I know she'll flip over it. Maybe today was a bust, but that doesn't mean this whole weekend has to be. Maybe I can still find the perfect moment to tell her after all. I mean, it took even Althena a few tries to understand what exactly there was between Charlie and her—twenty-three issues, to be exact.

Before we leave Javits to take the 5:35 p.m. train home, Roxana makes plans to meet up with Devin tomorrow. I try to ignore that this is happening by texting with Casey. He's staying until closing tonight, but we're going in again together tomorrow morning.

The day has turned sunny and warm for mid-October, so none of us even put on our jackets as we walk toward Penn Station. Felicia's phone buzzes and I catch her smiling as she looks at it.

"You guys, that was *so* much fun!" she says as she walks between Roxana and me, quickly texting something back. "I had no idea. Best people-watching I've had all year, and most everyone in there was, like, oozing so much energy. Now I can see why you look forward to it."

I grin at her, but Roxana can't help teasing her a little. "Don't sound so shocked that we look forward to something actually *fun*."

"That's not what I meant! I just thought I'd feel left out with all the insider stuff. You know," Felicia explains.

"Ah, but that's the beauty of NYCC," I butt in. "No one is left out. Everyone gets to be a freak in their own special way."

But this sentiment starts to wear off as we get closer to Seventh Avenue and I notice we're getting more strange stares. Felicia finally realizes that she forgot to take off her Wonder Woman costume and hastily puts on her jacket over it.

I don't like being stared at either, so I tell them I plan to change in the Penn Station bathroom, before we get on the train.

"Us too," Roxana agrees.

But getting to the station and down the escalators is a crowded, jostled affair. And once we finally do get down to the LIRR level, we can see that the line for the only set of bathrooms is out the door and down a hallway. Oh, geez. Today is definitely a day of getting thwarted by lines.

Roxy looks at her watch. "We can't miss this train. My parents . . ."

"We won't," I assure her. "We'll just have to brave looking like this for now."

We look up at the big board, find our platform for the 5:35 train to Huntington, and make our way down to it. The platform is packed with middle-aged office workers and the three of us stick out like sore thumbs, but there's no help for it.

The stares make me uncomfortable, and I assume at least Roxy feels the same way. But when I look over at her, she's staring into space. She's taken her wig off and is rubbing the back of her short hair with her hand. I wonder what she's thinking so hard about, and my stomach plummets when I realize I probably already know the answer: Devin.

The train comes and we get pushed and bumped into as we follow the herd. Somehow, Roxana ends up a few people behind Felicia and me. I see two seats together and rush to claim them with Felicia on my heels, but I keep standing until Roxana gets on too. I motion for her to come take the seat next to Felicia.

But she shakes her head and points to a lone seat on the other end of the car. I watch her as she settles down in it. She smiles and waves at me and then takes out her sketchbook and pencil.

I slowly sink into my seat. "Sorry," I say to Felicia. "I tried to get her to come over here. . . ."

Felicia smiles at me. "No worries, Graham. Will it be so bad to sit next to me for an hour?"

"Oh, no. Of course not. That—that's not what I meant," I stammer. "I just thought you'd prefer to sit next to her. . . ." I trail off.

She raises her eyebrows at me but doesn't say anything else. Her phone buzzes again and she fiddles with it for a few minutes. By the time the train has started to move, she's turned it to silent and put it away. She clears her throat.

"So you and the girl from speed dating . . . ," she begins.

"The girl?" I'm genuinely confused for a second before I remember Amelia talking to me outside the Zinc panel. "Oh, right. Amelia." I nod at Felicia's bag, where she's just put her phone. "Is that who the texts are from? Someone you met at speed dating?"

"Yeah," she says, looking down at her bag pensively. "They were nice."

"They? How many have texted you already?"

She shrugs. "A couple . . ."

Of course. I shake my head with a small grin. "Just a couple?" I tease.

"Maybe a few . . ."

I laugh. "That's 'cause the con still goes on for a few hours. I'm sure you'll hear from the rest soon."

"Okay, right," she says dismissively. "But about *you* and the girl you met. You think there might be a spark there?" She gives me a friendly, conspiratorial elbow in the side.

"Oh, no," I say immediately. "Not that she wasn't nice or anything . . ."

She stares at me, as if waiting for me to finish that sentence, but I don't. So after a moment, she takes it upon herself to finish it for me. "I get it." She sounds like she's choosing her words carefully. "She's no Roxana."

I start, and I can't tell if it's because of a bump in the train track, or because of the shock to my system. Probably the latter. "So you *do* know . . . ," I finally whisper to her. "Wait, is it super obvious?"

"Not *super* obvious," Felicia says kindly.

My mind reels. "Do you think Roxana knows?" I blurt out, and instantly realize I have no idea what I want the answer to be. If she does know, then I guess I won't need to plan a grand reveal for tomorrow after all. But then again, if she does know and has shown me no hint that she does . . . she clearly doesn't return my feelings. Like, at all.

Felicia shakes her head and quickly gives me at least one small reprieve. "Honestly, I don't think so. She's not cool enough to act so nonchalant around you if she did know."

"Of course she's cool," I say a tad defensively.

Felicia smiles at me. "That's not the definition I meant. I meant playing it cool. She wouldn't be able to know something like that and not get visibly nervous, you know? She's too sensitive."

"Oh," I respond. I should ask her if she thinks Roxana feels the same way about me. Or if she ever could. I should ask, but . . . I just can't. Sweat springs out on the bridge of my nose, right where my glasses hit. I feel moisture on my palms as I clench and unclench my fists. God, if I can't even ask this question of Roxana's friend, who's created this perfect opening for me, how the hell am I ever going to confess anything to Roxana herself? I look down at the train floor in frustration, focusing my attention on a sad, crumpled, almost-empty paper cup of lemon Italian ice.

"You know, in some ways, you guys make a lot of sense," Felicia finally says, answering my unasked question anyway. I tear my eyes away from the cup and see that she's eyeing me thoughtfully, carefully.

There is a long pause.

"But . . . ," I croak out.

"I don't know, Graham. I truly don't know if there is a but." She smiles kindly at me again and I let out a breath I didn't know I was holding. Felicia doesn't know the answer, which means . . . there's still hope. Because if the answer was definitely no, wouldn't Roxana's girl best friend know? And wouldn't she put me out of my misery?

"You've never, like, talked about it? About me?" I say quietly, finally feeling brave enough to ask.

"Not in that way," Felicia responds. "But to be honest, there are some things Roxana plays very close to the vest. And romance is definitely a top one. I've never really been able to get her to tell me much about any guy she's been crushing on. Not that I haven't tried!"

I smile a little in the direction of the Italian ice cup. Maybe things aren't so bleak after all.

Felicia tactfully changes the subject then, talking about how fun she thought the costume contest was. "Some of those outfits were just amazing," she says. "And by the way, I never knew Casey was so funny."

"Casey?" I ask. "Zucker?" He can be funny, but usually only the .01 percent of the population who understand all his references would find him so.

Felicia nods. "Yeah. We were in the same speed dating group and I asked him who his favorite teacher at school was. And he said Mr. Reuben, followed closely by ROSIE, who is the only one who empirically knows many answers and cannot be duped by personal charm or asshattery." Felicia giggles.

I laugh too. ROSIE is the artificial intelligence computer that the Robotics Club has been working on and improving for several years now. And unlike some of the teachers at school, ROSIE definitely suffers no fools, and has no soft spot for jocks or class clowns. An awkward academic's dream.

A few stops before ours, the seat across from us finally opens up and Felicia gets Roxana's attention and motions for her to come over. When she does, Roxana shows us the sketch she's been working on. A paranoid part of my mind has automatically assumed it'll be a dreamy rendition of Devin, but it's actually a few panels of Rewinder serving out detention in Master Pernicky's specially created box, which doesn't allow her to mess with time. I see Roxana has put in my line of dialogue in a thought bubble.

"I can only *rewind* time, not fast-forward it. So why would I want to keep reliving detention? Idiots!" Rewinder says as she stares scornfully at the punishment box.

I smile. The illustration looks even better and more whimsical than what I pictured in my head . . . as always. Now I just need Roxana to complete *our* story, to take my words and make them come to life like we were starring in our own panels.

At the train station in Huntington, we all quickly head to the bathroom to change out of our costumes. After all, the Afsaris just might get a tad suspicious if they saw their daughter come home from play rehearsal dressed as an alien-by-way-of-replicant. I give Roxy a once-over to make sure she got all her makeup off before we head outside to meet Felicia's brother, Emile, who's waiting for us in his Toyota Prius.

"Did you have a good time?" he asks, and we all tell him yes before thanking him for the ride.

He drops both me and Roxana off at my house and we say good-bye to Felicia, who thanks us again for the fun day. "I kind of wish I was going tomorrow, too," she calls out before she and Emile drive off.

Roxana laughs as we watch them go. "She really was shocked she had such a good time, wasn't she?"

I laugh too. "She probably had no idea nerd stuff could be so fun," I admit.

Roxana looks toward the end of the block, where she'll have to go to make it look like she got off the late bus. She takes in a deep breath.

"Just play it cool," I advise. "Don't talk about anything. It's just a normal day." As if I'm the world's foremost expert in lying, which I most certainly am not. But Roxana definitely isn't either, and lying to her parents is probably somewhere near the top of her "Things Roxana Hates" list. Today has definitely been a sacrifice on her part—especially since the Zinc panel didn't even happen.

She blows out more deep breaths and nods as I continue to say encouraging words, like she's a boxer and I'm her coach. She even feigns a little jog as she revs herself up to go home.

"Text me when you're in the clear," I say, finishing my speech. She salutes me and then heads off to the corner, giving me one final glance and wave before she turns it.

I have about twenty minutes to myself when I get home before Dad comes in—he must have been on the train right after me. Since Casey isn't around, I'm skipping out on our standing weekly Magic tournament, too. Which I guess means I'll be hanging out with the fam tonight.

A few minutes later, Lauren comes in, and I smell Mexican takeout this time. I make my way to the dining room around the same time that Drew and Callie come out of the woodwork with the smell of food.

"Hey!" My dad beams at me. "How was it?"

"Really fun," I say, and hand over the Peter Mayhew photo.

"Awesome," Dad says as he looks at it. "My collection is almost complete." He's been collecting *Star Wars* autographs from the original trilogy for a long time, even getting people like Alec Guinness before he died.

"I still can't believe Graham gets to go to Nerd Central instead of school," Callie loudly complains.

"Um, you've missed school for pep rally preparation," I point out.

"That's *different*. That's an actual extracurricular activity?" Sometimes Callie ends perfectly normal sentences with a question mark, and I've never quite been able to put my finger on why.

At any rate, I get a small jolt of happiness that one good thing came out of the Zinc fiasco today: I don't have to figure out how to set her up with Casey. 'Cause, let me just say, Callie McCullough would not find Casey's feelings about ROSIE to be the slightest bit hilarious.

I'm about to help myself to a serving of rice and beans when my phone buzzes. **All clear!** the message from Roxana says. I grin and am about to write her back when I see the dot, dot, dot that indicates she's typing another message.

Wanna come over for dinner? Zereshk polo tonight . . .

Sweet! My favorite dish with my favorite girl.

I make hurried excuses to my family, who don't seem too concerned that I won't be around to field insults about Comic Con, and then I practically skip across the backyard.

Chapter 13
DINNER AND A WEB VIDEO

"Yes, Mrs. Afsari," I call back as I walk through the mudroom to the kitchen.

A small woman with jet-black hair, still dressed in her smart business attire, is standing over a steaming pot of white and yellow rice. It smells heavenly.

I go over and give her one kiss on each cheek, the way I learned to do long ago. "I could smell the *zereshk* from my house," I say, pointing to the plump, crimson dried berries dotting her rice.

She smiles. "Of course you could, *shekamoo*," she teases. Another word I learned a long time ago, which roughly translates to "someone with a healthy appetite." It's hard for me to understand how someone could eat Mrs. Afsari's cooking and *not* have a healthy appetite.

I grin back. "Plates?" I nod to the cabinet where I know they keep their dishes.

She nods. "Please. Samira was supposed to set the table, but you know . . ." She rolls her eyes and I laugh.

Roxana's eleven-year-old sister is nowhere to be found when I take the plates out to the dining room. More likely than not, she's working on her fan fiction. And even though I indulged Mrs. Afsari in chastising her for shirking her household duties, I'm much more naturally aligned with Samira's compulsion to write. After all, I know what it's like to be lured by the siren song of the muse, whether that comes in the form of a superhero or a member of a boy band.

I've just finished setting the last place when Roxana comes bounding down the stairs, her hair wet from a shower. "Hey," she says to me brightly before heading to the kitchen to grab the silverware.

In a few minutes, Mr. and Mrs. Afsari and Mrs. Tehrani—Mrs. Afsari's mother—have all assembled in the dining room. I give Roxana's grandmother two kisses too and quickly glance into her eyes—they're lucid and twinkling, nothing like they were the night she gave us all a scare this summer. Satisfied, I move over to firmly shake Mr. Afsari's hand. His head is almost completely bald, but he compensates for it by sporting a luxuriant black mustache.

"So how was school?" He asks his obligatory question as we all take our seats.

"Good," I say, and immediately catch a look of panic flicking across Roxana's eyes. "Junior year is always a little tough," I go on, to give Roxana time to compose herself. "But I think we'll be okay as long as we keep up with the work."

Mr. Afsari nods solemnly. "It's very important that you both study hard." The Afsaris uprooted everything and moved from Iran when Roxana was one so that their daughter would have "more opportunities for a better life." It's a specific type of pressure that I know Roxana often feels acutely.

"Samira!" Mrs. Afsari is standing at the foot of the stairs, calling for her younger daughter. There's no answer, and then Mrs. Afsari calls again, adding a phrase in Farsi. I don't know what she's saying, but I can hear the exasperation in her voice.

"Coming!" Sam calls down.

Mrs. Afsari waits until she can hear footsteps on the stairs before giving a curt nod and heading back to her seat.

A rail-thin girl with long brown hair, almost as tall as her older sister, comes down the stairs, muttering to herself. She smiles when she looks up and sees me. "Oh, good!" she says as she comes to the table.

I share a conspiratorial grin with her. "How's the writing going?"

"I'm having third act problems!" she replies.

I nod solemnly. "Want to powwow later?"

"Oh my God. Please!" She grabs a seat as her mother spoons a heaping pile of rice onto her plate, followed by a golden piece of chicken and—the best part of any Persian meal—a slab of crispy rice called *tahdeeg*.

I'm salivating as Mrs. Afsari serves me up a portion.

"So, Graham, how did you do with your ranking? Was it a good number?" Mrs. Afsari asks, and it takes me a second to realize that— of course—we're still on the subject of school. "We're very proud of Roxana." She says Roxy's name the Persian way—the correct way, as it were, since they named her and all—with a long *o* and the emphasis on the first syllable. I've been secretly practicing saying it this way myself, but something about it feels so intimate that I've yet to break it out in front of Roxy. Maybe I can do one big reveal when I finally profess my real feelings. Sort of an *I love you and by the way I've figured out how to pronounce your name properly* one-two punch.

"I'm number eleven," I reply, and both the elder Afsaris beam at me.

"That's very good," Mrs. Afsari says as she rewards me with an extra piece of *tahdeeg*.

Samira barely conceals the roll of her eyes. I wink at her and she shakes her head. "Nerd," she mutters under her breath good-naturedly.

"Did I tell you Felicia is number one?" Roxana says, clearly happy to divert the conversation from what happened at school *today*.

I blink at her. Whoa. I'm going to have to let Casey know that. Although, really, we both should have guessed. Still, that's a tough break for him; it's going to be pretty near impossible to take Felicia Obayashi down.

"That's wonderful," Mrs. Afsari says. "Her parents must be so happy."

I'm sure Felicia's parents have nothing to complain about—ever—and I wonder if they constantly marvel at having such a perfect daughter or if they just take it for granted.

"I can't wait for Sunday." Samira changes the subject as she pushes some rice and *zereshk* into her spoon and takes a big mouthful. "They just added another fan fiction panel."

Sam is coming to NYCC with us on Sunday, which is the official kids' day, though I know most of the things she's interested in are the same things we are. Beside the writing panel, Aaron Dunning, who is one of her favorite celebrities and is also in one of my favorite movies, will be there, and we're both planning to get our photos taken with him.

"I wish I could go tomorrow, too," Samira says, shooting her mom a pointed glare. Samira has Persian school on Saturdays, something Roxy finally managed to convince her parents she could quit this year. But her little sister hasn't been so lucky yet.

"What will you be doing tomorrow?" Mrs. Afsari asks Roxana and me, ignoring her younger daughter's loud sigh.

"Just some writing and drawing panels. Getting some autographs. That sort of stuff." I don't want to elaborate and make Sam any more jealous than she already is.

Roxy's grandmother says something in Farsi. She's a small woman with laughing hazel eyes and short, perfectly coiffed, brassy blond hair. I've never heard her speak English but I know for a fact that she understands every word. (I have definitely caught her watching *Law & Order: SVU* marathons.) Roxy once told me her grandmother is embarrassed about getting words wrong so she prefers not to even try.

Memories flood my mind of how, a few months ago, I picked up the phone and heard Roxana's shaky, tear-filled voice. "My grandmother. Something's wrong. I called the hospital and the ambulance is coming. But my parents won't be home for a while."

"Be right over."

When I got there, Mrs. Tehrani was sitting in the same dining room chair she's sitting in now, but she was staring off into space, her eyes glassy and unfocused. She was muttering something. I assumed it was something in Farsi, but Roxana corrected me.

"I don't know what she's saying," she sobbed. "She keeps calling me Elham. That's the name of her daughter who died before my mom was born. But then she's speaking in Turkish, too. And I don't understand."

I pulled her in for a hug and then calmly—though I don't know where that calm came from—told her to go hold her grandmother's hand and just keep talking to her, letting her know she was there. Roxy did as I said, and then I sat in the chair next to her and held Roxy's other hand. Mrs. Tehrani continued to mutter to herself, Roxana kept murmuring close to her ear, and I just held on and let her squeeze my hand. When the ambulance came, the paramedics let us both ride with her. Our hands remained clasped together for the whole trip.

We weren't allowed to go farther than the waiting room while the doctors and nurses took over. It was another forty-five minutes before the rest of Roxana's family arrived. Her mom came first, then her dad, who had picked up Samira from summer camp. Roxana and I only let go of each other's hands about ten thirty that night, when we parted ways in her backyard.

The next day, her grandmother was released from the hospital. The doctors had tested for a stroke, a heart attack, and a myriad of other things. It might just be an isolated incident, they finally concluded. Otherwise, they had no answers. But somehow, when I woke up the next day, a different sort of answer had settled into my heart—one to a question I didn't know I was asking. I couldn't stop thinking about Roxana's tearstained cheek on my chest or the feel of her hand pressed into mine, which felt like clay that had hardened into permanence. I couldn't stop feeling a sense of pride and awe that I was the first person she'd called, that I got to be a strong and calming presence through something that was so terrifying for her—just like she was there for me after my mom died. Within days, my feelings had fermented and fortified until I finally had to acknowledge them for what they really were: I was head over heels in love.

"*Merci*, Mamanbazorg," Roxy says now, taking me out of my reverie and putting her hand lightly on her grandmother's. Then she turns to me to translate what Mrs. Tehrani just told her in Farsi. "She said that soon people will be lining up for our autographs at the convention."

I grin at Mrs. Tehrani, and she winks back at me. "*Merci, Khanoom Tehrani,*" I say, and her grin gets bigger. Roxana's family never seems to stop delighting at the five words of Farsi I've picked up over the years. And I can't say I tire of getting their stamp of approval, either.

"Show-off," Samira mutters, giving me a playful nudge, and then, louder so that her family can hear, "You sure you don't want to go to Farsi school instead of me tomorrow, Graham? You can learn *lots* of wonderful words there." I stick my tongue out at her when her family isn't looking.

After my third helping, I finally throw in the towel on trying to fit any more food into my stomach. We're clearing up the dinner plates when my phone buzzes.

It's a notification that someone has sent me a direct message through the Z-men message boards. It's a video message, and I realize after a second of staring at the sender's username who it must be from. Amelia.

"Oh my God," I say to Roxy. "It looks like she sent me a video."

"Who?"

"The girl I met at . . ." I almost say *speed dating*, but I catch myself just in time as her dad goes to take the salad dressing from where it's tucked under my arm. "That thing Felicia signed us up for," I finish, hoping that sounds vague enough to be misconstrued as school-related. "Can we go watch it on your computer?"

"Sure," Roxy says, and the two of us work double-time to finish loading the dishwasher before we race up to her room.

"This girl I met at speed dating had a Zinc wristband," I tell Roxy as we're firing up her computer. "I found out she's a Z-man, and she just sent me a video. I wonder if it's from the panel. . . ." I know that earlier I decided I didn't want to see or hear anything to do with this panel ever again, but things seem different now that it's just Roxy and me in her room, sharing in the anticipation of whatever this could be.

Being in Roxy's room gives me a pang lately. Of course I've been here hundreds of times before, but it only recently occurred to me that her parents probably wouldn't let her have any other boy up here. Maybe that should make me feel special, but instead, I have mixed feelings about it. Mostly because I think even her family doesn't consider me a real boy . . . not the kind who might have anything other than friendly designs on their daughter, that is.

We use my log-in on z-men.net and read the message together. Earhart5921 writes:

> They were very strict about camera phones. I tried
> to sneak in a longer video but was almost immedi-
> ately spotted by security and had to quickly hide my
> phone before I got kicked out. So I only have four
> seconds of video to share . . . I thought you might
> want to see it anyhow. Oh, and please don't share

this online or anything! I don't want it to somehow

get traced back to me. ~Amelia.

With trembling fingers, I click on the Play button of the attached video. "Hi, I'm Bob," a man with tidy gray hair and an unassuming blue polo shirt says before the image goes all lopsided and cuts to black.

Roxana and I stare at the computer screen and then at each other. Before I can think to do it, Roxana has rehit the Play button. Bob says hello from behind his table again. And again and again and again.

After we've watched it nearly twenty times, Roxana finally turns to me. "That was really him . . . ," she says.

"And he said something!" I continue. "He said his name!"

There hasn't been video of the man in twenty years. This is precious. This is sacred. And, for this moment, it is ours.

So we discuss it. How normal he looks. How soft-spoken. How no one would ever be able to tell that under that tuft of gray hair lies the brain of a creative genius. We find we can stretch that four seconds of video into an hour and a half of solid conversation, before I realize that I have to get home at some point tonight. Probably even the Afsaris have their limit as to how late a boy can be up in their daughter's room, even if that boy is just me.

That night at home, I write Amelia back to thank her profusely; it was beyond nice of her to do that for a stranger:

You are a prince (princess?) among Z-men. This
will probably be the highlight of my year. (Though
please don't ruin it for me by reminding me that the
highlight of YOUR year will actually be seeing Zinc
IN PERSON. ;-))

And then, lying in bed, I think about watching the video with Roxana, everything we've shared today and over the years. Out of the millions of memories, I pluck a shining one, when she first called me a Weasley, one of our earliest inside jokes. I never really minded because Ron was always my favorite character; he was the funny one. It's only now that I realize—he's also the one who got the girl.

I turn to my side and stare at my moon-splashed bookshelf. The two shelves that are exactly at my eyeline when I lie down are that way by design. They hold my mom's books, the ones she wrote. Four slim volumes of critical essays on the works of filmmakers John Hughes, Cameron Crowe, Amy Heckerling, and Nora Ephron. Next to them is her scrapbook of movie stubs and short reviews, which I've kept up and added to through the years with ones of my own. And then, surrounding them and on the shelf underneath, her DVDs. Not all her DVDs, because there were too many to fit on a bookshelf. Most of them remain boxed in our basement somewhere.

But her favorites. The ones that eventually became Roxana's favorites. And, of course, mine. Sometimes I feel like Roxana and my mom sharing their love of movies like *Sixteen Candles, Say Anything . . .*, *Clueless, When Harry Met Sally . . .* it's like they found a way to know each other beyond the grave.

I didn't get it at first when we were nine and Roxana saw the DVDs and asked if we could watch Mom's favorite movies. I didn't think it would come to mean anything. But when she just genuinely loved them, and she made me love them, it was, in a small way, like a piece of Mom was there—in her passions, which had found their way to becoming my best friend's passions too.

I think of all the romantic comedies my mom studied, critiqued, and wrote about. The really great ones. And I realize that tomorrow there are more chances to bring one of them to life. After all, the John Hughes retrospective and panel will be happening, and that ties Roxy and me together almost as much as Zinc does.

Tomorrow, I think as I drift off to sleep. *Tomorrow I will tell her.*

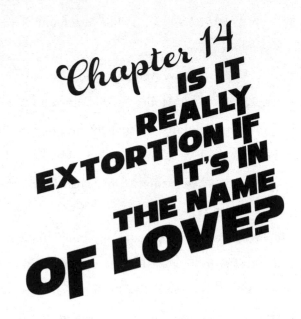

Chapter 14
IS IT REALLY EXTORTION IF IT'S IN THE NAME OF LOVE?

"AND YOU DIDN'T LOOK AT TODAY'S SCHEDULE, RIGHT?" I ASK ROXANA FOR THE third time.

She stops right in front of the glass doors, looks me straight in the eyes, and grabs me by the lapels of the mustard-yellow leather jacket I'm wearing on top of my Deadpool T-shirt. I was inspired to dig into my closet after reminiscing about our seventh-grade Halloween, but the jacket is the only part of Charlie Noth's outfit that still fits me— mostly because it was enormous on me back then and I can actually fill it out now, thankfully. "For the last time, Posner, no," Roxana says. "And can we talk about what kind of implicit trust I'm putting in you that I won't be missing anything crucial because you want to surprise me with something?"

I grin down at her. "You won't miss anything crucial. I promise."

"I better not." She pushes me away lightly.

"Guys, let's stand away from the door," Casey, ever cognizant of con protocol, chimes in. It's just us three here today, the true NYCC nerds.

"Hi!" a voice says, and I see Roxy's face immediately get simultaneously two shades brighter and pinker.

Oh. And I guess Devin.

He gives a hug to Roxy and a friendly wave to Casey and me, and it's only then that I realize Roxy may have taken more care than usual with her appearance. There's no cosplay for her today. She's wearing a red polka-dotted dress instead of her normal T-shirt and jeans. It's not even a comic-related dress, unless she's going for a Minnie Mouse vibe, I think uncharitably. She's also wearing a bit more makeup than usual . . . not that she needs it.

"You would be proud to know that I read the first three issues of *Althena* last night. Downloaded them as soon as I got home," Devin says to Roxana, and her face brightens up even more.

"And . . ." She coaxes out his response.

"Brilliant, of course. You were right." He turns to me and grins, and I barely muster a sarcastic smile back. Like I really need his stamp of approval on just my very favorite thing ever.

Devin turns back to his rapt audience instead. "The story is wonderful, but his color work . . ."

"Oh. My. God. I know, right?"

"I mean, how does he get it to be so luminous? I was trying to figure out the medium—"

"It's gouache," Roxana interrupts him.

"Gouache? No."

"Oh, yes. Zinc was one of the first to popularize paint in sequential art." Roxana nods vigorously and they immediately go on to have a deep discussion about Zinc's use of cadmium yellow.

I stand there agape and useless, and it's only Casey's adherence to his schedule that finally gets us out of this nightmare discussion. He has a video game reveal he wants to get to in ten minutes, and the original plan was for me and Roxana to tag along. Of course, now we have a tall British boy-shaped tumor with us too.

Casey and I end up leading the way to the Electronic Arts booth. I hear Devin telling Roxana all he's planning for today, but I'm too wrapped up in my own dark thoughts to realize he's holding a schedule in front of her.

"I'm not sure what to do at five p.m.," he's saying. "There's a couple of cool things. Probably the Adult Swim panel. But there's also a John Hughes retrospective—"

"WHAT?" Roxana practically screams, and I stop dead in my tracks causing her to bump into me.

I turn around slowly and see her eyes shining brightly at me. "Oh, Graham! That's the surprise, isn't it?"

I swallow hard. All this time I managed to keep it a secret. *All this time.* I turn to Devin, and never before have I wished so hard to have Cyclops's optic blast ability at my disposal.

But Roxana is squealing and hugging me and I have to bury my resentment quickly. "Yeah," I croak out. "That was it."

"Oh, Graham! That's amazing. Wait, can I see the schedule now?"

I shrug my assent because what does it really matter at this point, and Roxana grabs the schedule from Devin.

"So I take it you're a fan?" Devin grins rakishly, but for once Roxana ignores him.

"Oh my gosh. 'Molly Ringwald, Jon Cryer, Anthony Michael Hall, Andrew McCarthy, and *Pretty in Pink* director Howard Deutch discuss the work of the venerable writer/director/producer John Hughes—the godfather of teen romantic comedies. To be followed by a screening of *Pretty in Pink*,'" she reads. "That is amazing!" She grins up at me, and it's hard in that moment not to smile back.

"I put the panel in my schedule too," Casey says. "Though I'll have to skip the screening."

I look at Casey confusedly as we get back in step to head toward the game reveal. "Really? I didn't think that panel would really be your scene."

Casey looks back at Roxana in as unstealthy a way as possible and sees that she's once again in discussion with Devin, before stepping a bit closer to me and whispering, "Well, isn't that where you're going to tell her?"

"I . . ." I do a quick check back to Roxy too and catch her and Devin laughing together. "Don't know," I finally finish truthfully. "But wait. You want to be there for that?"

Casey shrugs. "Honestly, there just happens to be nothing else that interesting going on at the time, so I figured why not. Plus Hughes is cool. And oh, I thought maybe I could pick up some pointers. You know, in case Callie and I ever happen."

Wow. I can't believe he's still on that. "Why do you like her so much?" I blurt out.

"She's hot. Don't you think?"

"Gross. No, I don't think that."

"Well, if she wasn't your stepsister, you would," he says firmly.

We've now finally gotten to the EA booth and found some room to stand in the back while we wait for the preview to start. "Okay, fine. Let's say, objectively, you're right and she's attractive. You guys have *nothing* in common. Believe me, I know. Because she and I have nothing in common."

Casey considers this for a second. "Is that what you really think it's all about? Having things in common?"

"Of course!" I practically shout before catching myself and quickly glancing around at Roxy, who is, luckily, still not paying attention to us. "I mean, after all the physical stuff, you do actually have to talk to them, you know," I say more quietly.

"But, I mean, do you think it's so great to have *everything* in common?

Shouldn't you have a few different interests?" He nods back toward Roxy, and I scowl.

"We have some different interests," I mutter.

He looks at me dubiously. "Like British guys," he says without preamble. Or, unfortunately, malice.

I grit my teeth and lightly shove him anyway. "Uncool, dude. And why would I take love advice from you, by the by?"

He shrugs, unfazed. "Fair point."

The presentation starts then and we spend the next twenty minutes watching some ultraviolent but beautifully rendered cut scenes and a demo of the gameplay. Then the audience is invited to stand in what is looking to be a two-to-three-hour line for the opportunity to slaughter some aliens in glorious Ultra HD for five minutes.

"What do you think? Should we brave the line?" Devin asks.

I expect Roxana to say no way, but she just nods brightly. "Sure!"

Really? I know for a fact there are hundreds of things here that would be way more her speed than *Mars Massacre.*

"Hey, Graham. Don't you have that Building Characters panel in fifteen minutes?" Casey asks.

I do, and one of my favorite writers is going to be talking craft there, but . . . I don't think I should leave Roxana and Devin alone together *yet again.*

"Oh! Is that the one with Suellen Ling?" Roxana asks before I get a chance to divulge my plans to skip the panel.

"Yup," Casey responds. "It's actually on my schedule too. It's a really great lineup. Peterson-Davitz is also gonna be there."

Great. Now I can't back out without it looking too suspicious. Roxy knows this is a convention highlight for me.

"So see you later, then?" Roxana says brightly, and I mutely nod, cursing Ling and Peterson-Davitz and, most especially, Casey Zucker right now.

It's only as Casey starts walking away and I feel obliged to follow him that I remember to at least make plans to meet up again. "Meet you back here at noon?" I call out to Roxana, unwisely walking backward across the crowded show floor.

"You got it," she calls out, and I turn around about 2.5 seconds away from walking into, and possibly demolishing, an enormous homemade Optimus Prime consisting mostly of cardboard. I mutter an apology but get cursed out anyway as I follow in Casey's wake.

Saturday is understandably one of the convention's busiest days, so the floor is even more packed than yesterday. We're trickling along behind a group of six or seven Tetris blocks who keep getting stopped so that people can take their photos. But every time we try to pass them, we're thwarted by a Spidey or Leia or their ilk heading in the other direction.

The third time we get blockblocked (the new term I just coined for being barricaded by a 1980s video game graphic), I let out a loud sigh that fogs up the glass of the booth I happen to be standing next to. I peer into the case as my breath dissipates.

And there, appearing as if out of the fog machine of a Whitesnake music video, is a small collection of Zinc memorabilia. Two original covers and an original page. They each have a price tag on them. The covers say they're starting at the exorbitant price of $1,500, while the page starts at a slightly more reasonable $500. I take a closer look at the page and my heart nearly stops. Holy crud. It's from Roxana's favorite issue, the penultimate one of the *Althena* series. It's also probably Althena and Charlie's most romantic scene, at the moment when Althena is called back to her planet and Charlie realizes she's about to be gone forever. That's when he says the line about her being the most beautiful thing he's never seen. It's the closest they ever came to saying "I love you."

I look up at the booth and see the sign then: SUN AUCTIONS. ORIGINAL COMIC ART AUCTION SUNDAY AT 3:30 P.M.

"I have to buy this," I mutter to really no one, though I eventually realize that Casey is still beside me. So I turn to him and reiterate my vow. "I have to."

This is it. The Zinc panel didn't pan out. And my John Hughes surprise is ruined. But I'll buy this, and then I'll say to Roxy, "Imagine it's me and you on this page. You're Althena and I'm Charlie. Only instead of me *almost* saying 'I love you,' I'm here, saying it to you for real." I picture it perfectly. After the auction. The two of us in an empty conference room here at NYCC. Me presenting her with the page (enclosed in a hard plastic case, of course), her falling into my arms, the music swelling . . .

"Um, do you have five hundred dollars?" As per usual, Casey, dasher of dreams, is at it again. He's squinting into the case now too.

"Not at the moment," I start out slowly, but thinking fast. "But . . ."

"And remember, it starts at five hundred. Who knows how high it'll actually get?"

He's right, but my brain is already ahead of him. Only one person I know has that kind of money: Casey himself. He's been investing his bar mitzvah money for years, saving up for his Ivy League education.

So I start beseeching. I promise him everything I already promised him if we got the Zinc wristbands—including trying to set up the date with Callie—plus I tell him I'll pay him back with interest over the next two years. "By the time you start your freshman year at Harvard or Yale or Princeton, you will have all your money back. I swear."

"How are you going to do that?"

"I'll get a job. I'll work day and night if I have to. Please, Case. Please?"

But he's shaking his head at me with something like incredulity. "Dude. You're obsessed." This is rich coming from someone who's fluent in both the Sindarin and Quenya tongues of Elvish.

But then I remember the one other card I have, my ace in the hole, so to speak. And I decide to play it. "I know who's currently ranked number one in the class."

He visibly starts. "Who is it?" he asks wildly.

"If you lend me the money, I'll tell you," I say calmly.

His eyes narrow. "After all we've been through, it all boils down to extortion, then?"

I feel a little bad. But not too bad. Because this is a negotiation, after all. So I simply stare at him.

He stares back.

We stand at a stalemate as he waits to see if I'm going to spill the beans. But alas, the silence seems to get to him before it gets to me. "I'll . . . think about it," he finally says darkly. "But we have to run. We're going to miss the panel."

My mind works furiously all the way to the panel as I realize I'm probably going to have to go through with my room-switching plan with Callie after all. I also start racking my brain for places I want to start working. Maybe Halfling Comics at the mall? That wouldn't be so bad, and I'd get a sweet discount. Plus I'm already there most Friday nights anyway for our Magic tournaments.

I'm smiling by the time we file into the panel room. Because I will get the money and buy the page and this will all happen exactly like the scene I just wrote in my head.

Chapter 15
AND HE SAID UNTO THEM . . .

LUCKILY THE BUILDING CHARACTERS PANEL ISN'T TOO PACKED AND WE SNAG
seats near the back without a problem. Before the panel starts, I hear
someone call my name.

It's Amelia. She's wearing a Young Guns Press T-shirt today, her curly
hair with its red streak wild and free. I grin at her, immediately remembering the video from last night.

"Hi!" I say enthusiastically. "Listen, thank you again for the video.
I don't know if my message adequately conveyed how grateful I really
am."

"Dude. I really am so sorry you missed it. That was cruel and unusual punishment for a true Althena fan." She points to an empty seat next to us. "Mind if I sit with you?"

"Of course not," I say, and while she settles down I think to introduce her and Casey. "Amelia got into the Zinc panel yesterday," I explain.

"Details?" Casey asks.

"It. Was. Awesome," Amelia gushes. "Like, so awesome, I took notes."

"You did?" I ask.

"Yup. How else am I going to do a proper postcon analysis?" she says with a grin.

I laugh, and Casey looks both impressed and like he's calculating something. "Hey, do you think you'd be willing to share your notes with us?" He roots around in his backpack and takes out his spreadsheet. "If you have some time at . . . noon. Or three thirty? Or six forty-five?"

Amelia looks over Casey's paper, and now it's her turn to look impressed. And perhaps slightly alarmed, but who can blame her? "Wow. That's one well-thought-out schedule," she says diplomatically.

"Thank you," Casey responds.

"And the answer is yes. I'd definitely be up for telling you guys what went down yesterday."

She smiles at me again, and I get a burst of inspiration. "What about noon?" I ask. "Would you be free for lunch or something after this? We have a friend who would *love* to hear about this too. I wouldn't want her to miss it."

"Oh, sure."

"Hi, and welcome to the Building Characters panel, everyone." A voice comes over the speakers, and we turn our attention back to the three people sitting at the front of the room.

Forty minutes and some excellent writing advice later, we all clap for the panel and start to gather our backpacks and file out.

"Do you do character profiles?" Amelia asks me.

"Not really. But I might have to now," I respond. "By the way, what's with wearing the Enemy's T-shirt?" I raise my eyebrows and point to the logo of *Althena*'s publisher that's emblazoned on her top.

She looks down and laughs. "Yesterday was an exoneration. I think Bob would be okay with this."

"Bob?"

"Yes, we are on a first-name basis now, thank you."

Outside, we get caught in the flow of the crowd and don't have much of a chance to talk as we walk almost single file back to the Electronic Arts booth. When we find Roxana and Devin, they're about five people away from the front of the line.

"Wow, you guys still haven't gotten to the game?" I ask.

"No, but that's all right. The company was excellent," Devin says, grinning at Roxana, obviously reminiscing about any number of riveting conversation they've enjoyed over the past hour. Whatever, Stud Crumpet. Soon I will be the one with the ultimate weapon: the Zinc page.

"Hi, I'm Amelia." She sticks her hand out to Roxy and Devin and they both introduce themselves.

"Amelia is the one who sent me the video last night," I tell Roxana by way of explanation, and her face lights up.

"Oh, awesome!" Roxana says.

"And she said she'd tell us more about the panel. So I was thinking . . . lunch?"

"Oh . . ." Devin looks wistfully at the front of the line.

"I have about fifty minutes before I have to be back for another panel," Casey, bless him, chimes in.

"Me too," Amelia says. "I have something in an hour."

"Then let's do lunch now," Roxana says, her eyes shining with curiosity. "I mean, you don't really mind, do you, Devin?"

"Oh. No, that's okay." Devin, unfortunately, quickly recovers from his obvious disappointment and doesn't throw an enormous tantrum that would immediately point out to Roxana and everyone else in our hearing range that he is clearly the wrong guy for her. Damn him.

"Food court?" Casey asks.

"Actually, there's a pretty good diner just a couple of blocks from here," Amelia pipes up. "If you feel like venturing out."

We all agree, and Amelia leads the way out of the Javits and one avenue over to a big diner where most of the patrons are also costumed and/or wearing laminated badges around their necks.

We manage to grab a booth and have just put in an order for sodas when Casey decisively shuts his menu and turns to Amelia. "So, um, you know what you want?"

Amelia scans the menu for a few seconds. "Hmmm . . . I'm kinda feeling like breakfast, actually. Maybe the banana walnut pancakes."

"Great!" Casey enthuses before switching over to a much more serious voice. "Ready to talk about the panel, then?"

Amelia laughs before closing her menu too. "Sure. Hold on. I'll get this as accurate as possible for you." She shoots me a smile before reaching into her backpack and grabbing a small spiral notebook that I recognize as the type reporters usually use; I actually carry a similar one for impromptu writing sessions. She opens it, scans a page, and then looks back up at us.

"Okay. So he was already sitting there when we all filed in! Robert Zinc. Like he definitely didn't want any big entrance or anything. So it was kind of super quiet as everyone took their seats. We were all just watching this middle-aged guy in a blue polo shirt, sipping his water and chatting quietly with Solomon Pierce-Johnson, and we were all trying to catch his murmured words. Like he was some sort of prophet, you know?"

The waitress comes over then and we all hurriedly give our orders. I just order whatever Casey does because I definitely have no time to concentrate on something as prosaic as lunch right now.

When the waitress goes away again, we turn our rapt attention back to Amelia.

"So we were told immediately that there would be no Q&A session, just the carefully curated questions Solomon already had. Then Bob introduced himself . . ." Amelia looks pointedly over at me, referencing her miraculous little video, and I nod in recognition. "And Solomon began," she says, looking down at her notes again.

"So there were a few softball questions," she continues. "You know, 'How did you get your start?' And 'Where did the inspiration for Althena come from?' Stuff everyone there already knew."

Roxana and I exchange a glance, and I feel like both of us can conjure up exactly the words "Bob" used to answer those questions in his quiet, measured away.

"But then . . . ," Amelia says, and stares at each of us around the table in turn, as if she's Hercule Poirot about to accuse the murderer at last. "Solomon asks him, 'What really happened between you and Young Guns?'" And as if on cue, there's a collective gasp around the table.

Of course, just then the waitress comes back with our plates of food and I find myself annoyed that any of us ordered anything at all. It doesn't help that Devin asks for ketchup and keeps us waiting even longer until she's gone and everyone is settled. Devin digs in immediately, but the rest of us don't even pick up our utensils as we wait for Amelia to continue the story.

"'What really happened between you and Young Guns?'" She recaps for us like we just came back from a commercial break. "And that's when Bob says . . . Wait, I want to get this as right as I possibly can." She looks down at her notebook and reads to us from it. "He says, 'To be honest with you, I think I was a bit of a pretentious ass. I do think Young Guns could have stood to throw a little more money and publicity my way, but I think I honestly could have easily negotiated for that. It got a little too personal between me and Adam Warren. I'm guessing many of you might know, we exchanged some words back then.'"

Amelia looks up at us, as I imagine Zinc looked up at the audience, and we stare back at her aghast in the same way I'm sure they did yesterday. There were a couple of legendary e-mails between Warren, the president of Young Guns, and Zinc that had never entirely been proven to be authentic. But because they contained some seriously creative swearing, any Zinc fan over the age of ten had pored over them and possibly even incorporated some choice phrases into their vocabulary. I still use *crusty unicorn balls* on occasion.

And now here he was, finally confirming their veracity.

"He went on," Amelia says, and we all just nod, entranced. "He said, 'Adam and I had some personal issues with each other.'"

"His wife?" Casey butts in. That was the rumor, that Zinc had slept with Warren's wife.

Amelia shakes her head. "Sorry, chief. Did not get a confirmation on that point. But he continued, 'But I never should have let that affect the work. At the end of the day, Adam Warren respected *Althena*. His editorial notes always made the work stronger. I think, honestly, we could have made a few more years of really solid issues together.'"

Amelia stops there and stares at each of us in turn again.

"Son of a bitch," I mutter under my breath. "A few more years of *Althena*?"

Amelia nods. "Not only that, but Zinc went on to say he had a lot of those story arcs outlined. He *knew* what was going to happen."

"Oh my God," Roxana says. "So Althena was going to come back?" In the last issue Althena heartbreakingly went back to Ezula, and as far as the Zinc canon went, Charlie never saw or heard from her again. **"Every night, I dream about a different face,"** he says. **"Every morning, I wake up knowing it was her."**

Amelia shakes her head sadly. "He didn't confirm that, either. But I think we can assume . . ."

We all just sit there in near silence, except for Devin, who is still stabbing at his omelet with a fork. The waitress comes back around and glances at our untouched food. "Is everything okay?" she asks us.

"Oh, yeah. Sure," we all mutter, and limply pick up our utensils at last. Amelia takes a bite of her pancakes before thankfully starting to speak again.

"That was kind of the biggest revelation," she says. "He didn't elaborate from there, and Solomon didn't press him. . . ." She rolls her eyes. "And, of course, there was no Q&A session. Though I could've sworn there were people eyeing Solomon's mic like they were thinking about organizing an impromptu takeover." She chews another bite of her food and swallows before continuing. "The rest of the questions mostly had to do with the movie. Zinc said he had seen some of the dailies and was very happy with how it was coming along so far."

"Well, of course he would have to say that with the director sitting right there," Casey astutely points out.

Amelia nods. "Totally." She looks down at her notebook again. "Oh! And Solomon asked him one other really great question, I thought. About gender identity, and how *Althena* was really far ahead of its time in that regard."

One of the most interesting things about Althena's alien species is that they don't have two genders, they have fifty-seven to choose from. In fact, it's one of the things that fascinates and amuses Althena the most about humans, being limited to only two and being so staunch about how they get paired up. Throughout the series, Althena herself changes back and forth between male and female human forms pretty constantly. And, of course, Charlie falls in love with her anyway.

"What did Zinc say?" I ask Amelia.

"He said it was of course a conscious decision on his part. Things were different back in the early nineties, especially with the AIDS epidemic, and there was a lot of fear about homosexuality and transgender people and just . . . anyone who was different. Living in Greenwich Village, he saw how it affected so many people he knew and was friends with. And one day he just wondered, if an alien species came down here, would they find this whole obsession with gender norms so absurd?"

"Wow," I say.

"Wow," Roxana repeats, and we stare at each other. It's always pretty amazing to find a new reason to put one of your idols up on an even higher pedestal.

"Yup," Amelia says. "The whole thing was really amazing. I mean, even more so . . . not to be disappointed, you know? That something you built up for so long was even better than what you'd imagined?"

We all nod, completely understanding the nerdticipation that all too often leads to an enormous letdown—usually hashed out in message boards and comments sections across the great World Wide Web. So to have something—or in this case, someone—live up to impossible expectations is a real cause for celebration.

Amelia tells us that Zinc left the stage then and they made everyone file out, so she has no idea where he went afterward.

"Sounds great!" Devin says too brightly, breaking our enchantment, because, of course, he hasn't been waiting years and years to hear some of these sacred revelations. I sneak a look at Roxy, who looks dazed at being pulled out of Amelia's story. "Shall we get the check?"

With the spell lifted, Casey realizes that he does have to get going to make it to his panel. So we wolf down some food, pay, and make our way back over to the Javits.

Chapter 16
A BRIEF HISTORY OF GEEKDOM

"I LIED," AMELIA SAYS AS SHE GLANCES AT HER PHONE. "MY NEXT PANEL doesn't start for another forty-five minutes, actually." She looks up at me and smiles.

"Ah, cool," I say, meaning it. We're now roaming the Block behind Roxana and Devin. This is kind of the random section of NYCC, where a lot of vendors are hawking their wares and there are lots of neat toys and objects to look at. The booth we're just walking by, for example, has something called 8-bit pixel art, where all the objects—from portraits to crossed swords—look like they come straight from a very early video game. I point out a particularly cool-looking Batmobile to Amelia.

"Awesome," she says, and then turns to me. "Okay, so Burton *Batman* or Nolan *Batman*?" She has a mischievous gleam in her eye that I don't understand because this is sort of a no-brainer.

"Um, Nolan?" I say, which is, of course, the obvious choice.

"See, I prefer Burton!" she exclaims, clearly delighted that I went with the other option so that she can explain her argument. Which, naturally, I make her do. "I just think there's a certain playfulness with Burton that mirrors the original intention of the series. The dark stuff is there, but more subversive. I really like that."

"Yeah, but Nolan also ushered in this era of the true, dark superhero movie," I counter. "There's so much depth to it."

"But a lot of the humor is gone," she argues. "And Michael Keaton? Such a bold, unusual choice for Batman. But it so works."

"Oh . . . I see what's going on here," I say slowly. "You're a hipster nerd."

"Ha ha, very funny," she responds, but I can see she's genuinely amused. "And what kind of nerd are you, then?"

"Oh, I'm definitely an all-arounder," I immediately answer, because I have given this a lot of thought. "I'm kinda into it all. Comic books, regular books, movies, video games, television. Also, you know, like, actual school."

"Show-off." She's raising her eyebrows at me. "Isn't it funny, though? How it's become kinda cool to self-identify as a nerd? I doubt our parents had that luxury."

"They definitely didn't," I say before going on to explain about my OG dad. "He's got some stories that are straight out of, like, an episode of *Saved by the Bell*. I'm pretty sure there was a Kick Me sign involved."

Amelia laughs. "No way."

I nod. "The way he tells it, it's a miracle he ever met and married a woman. A miracle that I'm even here. But get this, you want to know how he got the nerve to speak to my mom?"

"How?"

"They were in college by then, mind you, so I think things were a little better. But he's in the park in the middle of campus, and he sees this pretty girl carrying this enormous book about . . . wait for it . . . *Star Wars*. And he realizes if he can't get up the nerve to talk to *her*, then he is just a completely hopeless cause. So he gathers up all his courage and he marches over to her and does the impossible: strikes up a flirtatious conversation."

Amelia smiles. "That's so cute!"

"Yes, trust me. It was a real triumphant moment for him. Of course, the real kicker is that she was carrying that book because she was a cinema studies major, not because she was a huge fan or anything."

Amelia laughs. "But he stuck with it anyway?"

I nod. "The OG may have been a shy nerd, but he's also a stubborn one."

"That's a really great story."

I nod. It is. I never tire of it, and after Mom was gone, I'd sometimes make my dad tell it to me at night, even when I was maybe too old for bedtime stories.

"And that's so cool about your mom," Amelia continues. "I've actually been considering going to film school myself."

"Really?" I ask.

"Excuse me." A voice interrupts our conversation. A short girl in a Superman shirt is smiling at us and brandishing a microphone. She gives me the once-over and then seems to be staring at Amelia's chest, which is a little bit disconcerting.

"I run a podcast, and we're doing a special Zinc fandom compendium," she explains. "Would you mind if I interview you?" She points toward Amelia again, and it's only then that I realize she's been observing Amelia's T-shirt. "If you're a fan, that is."

Amelia looks at me and I shrug. "Sure," she says. "And yup, we're fans."

I look ahead and see Roxy and Devin exiting the Block, not noticing that we've been held up. I don't want to lose sight of them, but it would be rude to leave Amelia now, so I just make a plan to text Roxy and catch up with her again as soon as this is over.

"Great!" the podcast host says. She turns on the little recorder attached to her microphone, looks down at some notes in her phone, and then looks back up at Amelia with a plastered smile. "A few easy ones. So do you think Zinc was well represented at New York Comic Con this year?"

"Um, well, he was actually here. Which has never happened before. So I would say yes," Amelia responds, throwing me a quizzical look. I shrug.

"Great," the girl says. "And how much of Zinc's work would you say you've read? Like what percentage?"

"One hundred," Amelia says.

"Really?" the girl asks.

"Well, there really isn't much of it," Amelia responds, throwing me another look. "Unless you're counting unpublished pieces . . ."

"No, no. Got it. You're a *huge* fan." The girl says the word *fan* as if she really wants to say *nerd* . . . and not in a cool twenty-first-century way, but kind of like she's a mean girl in one of my mom's eighties DVDs.

She looks up at Amelia again, and this time there's something piercing in her gaze, like she's a hard-hitting journalist about to throw a real curveball. "So if an alien came down to earth today, what do you think he or she would find most disconcerting about our legal system? Would it be pertaining to gun control, immigration, health care, or something else?"

This time Amelia shoots me a fully alarmed look. "Er, what?"

The girl doesn't flinch. "If, like in your favorite fantasy story, an alien came down to earth," she says more slowly, as if Amelia didn't comprehend the question because of how fast she was talking, "what—"

But Amelia stops her. "Um, okay. Right, I got the question." She thinks for a second. "I'm not a legal expert and I don't really see what this has to do with Zinc, to be honest, but I do think our gun control system is pretty broken."

"And how would you fix it?" the girl immediately asks. "I mean . . ." She stares down at her notes. "How would this alien maybe think to fix it?"

Amelia gamely and astutely answers a couple more in the girl's bizarre line of questioning, before cleverly saying she has another panel to get to.

"Me too." I jump on her gravy train when the girl looks as if she's about to start in on me.

As soon as we're out of earshot, Amelia turns to me and laughs.

"What was that?" I ask.

"I don't know, but sneak-attack politics at Comic Con is a little low, don't you think? Especially if you've clearly never even read your gateway series of choice."

"And obviously think it's beneath you," I point out.

Amelia rolls her eyes.

"Um, amazing answers, by the way," I have to say to her. "If she'd cornered me, I think I would've made a run for it."

"Ha! Thanks. I try to keep up with the news and have opinions on things, you know?"

I nod, a little awestruck. I have opinions on things too, but few of those things are part of what most would consider the real world.

I'm about to ask Amelia to tell me more about her interest in film school when a peculiar movement catches the corner of my eye.

We're a few feet down from the pixel art booth, and when I look over, I see a tall, muscular guy with shoulder-length dirty-blond hair about to scamper away from it. The thing I could have sworn I just saw him do is something very strange: tuck a sword into his pants like there was a scabbard there.

Normally, I wouldn't think twice about anyone carrying a sword at Comic Con as part of a costume. But this guy is dressed in nondescript baggy jeans, an oversized sweatshirt, and a Yankees cap. Not to mention there's just something about the way he's skulking away that seems . . . off.

More out of curiosity than anything, I find myself drawn back to the booth. "I just want to check something," I say to Amelia as I quickly walk over. She follows me.

"Excuse me," I say to the girl behind the counter when I get there. "Weird question. But, um, did you just sell a Master Sword?" I'm looking at the display case in front, where Amelia and I were just admiring a life-sized Zelda sword beautifully rendered from hundreds of tiny pieces of plastic. It was priced at $900 and is not there now.

The girl, who has dark hair and thick, sculpted eyebrows and doesn't look much older than me, glances down at the case, and her eyes grow wide. She mutters something under her breath that sounds like it might be a curse in a foreign language, and then she looks up at me. Her heavy eyebrows furrow in an accusatory scowl. "You take?" she asks angrily.

I put my hand up. "No, no!" I say. I look around and see the guy in the Yankees cap still ambling along, about to reach the end of the Block. "I think I saw him take it," I say.

She frowns as she looks down the aisle.

"Well, come on, then! Let's go catch up with him," a voice next to me says, and suddenly Amelia is jetting off after the guy.

"Wait!" I immediately run after her, but as we get closer to the guy, I can hear my pulse throbbing near my eardrum. Oh my God, what is she doing? And what are we going to do once we catch up to this guy? Confront him?

Amelia reaches him first, and she touches his elbow to get his attention. "Hey!" she says angrily. He turns around and stares down at Amelia, and I realize he looks far, far scarier up close. He's at least a foot taller than her—he's a few inches taller than me—and he looks decidedly mean. He has small blue eyes, a scraggly goatee, and a deep, ugly scar running down each side of his face.

He's glaring at Amelia, and with my eyes on his scars, I yell the first thing that comes into my head. "Hello! My name is Inigo Montoya. You killed my father. Prepare to die."

When I say I yell it, I mean it. I swear, half the con comes to a halt, staring at me. There's almost a hush in the Javits, and I think I can hear my line of regurgitated dialogue reverberate along the metal bars of the high ceilings.

"Is this like Comic Con theater?" I hear someone whisper.

"Shhh . . . I caught it on my phone!" someone else responds.

Meanwhile, the thief's glare is jumping up about ten notches in the menacing department and I have a feeling I'm about to pay for my knee-jerk—or should I say nerd-jerk—reaction to his face.

But then we hear footsteps behind us. "He stole sword." I look up to see the girl from the pixel art booth behind me. And she, thankfully, has a burly security guard with her.

"I didn't do nothing," the guy says right away, still staring at me as if he's memorizing my face.

"He saw," the girl says, pointing at me.

I'm sure my cheeks are about the color of Superman's briefs right now, but I think it's too late to back down at this point. "I think he put it in his pants," I mumble to the guard.

He looks at Scarface. "Okay. Are you going to show us, or do we need to have a pat-down?"

The guy sends one more angry look in my direction before reaching down and removing the sword from his pants. For a second, I'm actually scared he might run me through with it, before I realize that it is, in fact, plastic and that there are about a thousand witnesses.

"Okay, come with me," the guard says to the guy, grabbing his arm. He turns to the booth girl. "Do you want to press charges?"

The girl nods emphatically.

"Okay, then follow me to the security office," the guard says before looking at Amelia and me. "I don't think we'll need the two of you."

He starts to lead Scarface away.

"Thank you," the booth girl says to me with a big grin. "That was very important, expensive piece."

I nod at her with a sheepish smile and then, realizing people are still staring, clear my throat and start to walk quickly away in the other direction.

"Wait. Here. Take this as thank-you." She lifts something from around her neck and places it in my hand. It's a necklace made to look like three 8-bit heart containers in a row, the last heart only half full.

"Oh, that's not necessary . . . ," I start.

But the booth girl merely grins. "You can give to your girl," she says, before turning on her heels and running to catch up to the security guard.

From my side, I hear a gurgle of uncontrollable laughter.

I turn to see Amelia nearly doubled over from the giggles. "I cannot believe," she manages between fits, "that you just stopped a thief . . . with a *Princess Bride* line."

"It just . . . came out," I say, laughing now too as we exit the Block. "I saw the scars on the side of his face and the goatee . . ."

"And the first thing you thought of was Count Rugen?"

"Um. Yes."

She laughs loudly again. "I freakin' love it. You totally win the nerd card today. And not in a *Saved by the Bell* way."

She's beaming at me, and I can't help but grin back.

Then she takes out her phone and looks at it. "Oh, man. I have to go. I know you probably think I'm a loner nerd and all, just tagging along with you, but I am actually meeting some friends now before my next panel starts."

"Oh, yeah. That's exactly the vibe that comes across with you," I respond, in what I hope is clearly a sarcastic manner. "Loner nerd. Ready to tackle a thief who's twice her size at a moment's notice."

Her smile gets wider. "Tackle? Maybe. But defeat with classic movie lines? That is *much* more impressive." She puts her phone away. "Hey, do you want to come with? My friends are pretty awesome. Just like your group."

"Oh, thanks!" I say. "But speaking of which, I actually should go find Roxana and Casey. You know, I can't be the douche who just bounces the second another shiny new nerd comes along."

"Very noble," Amelia says. "Can I get your number, then? Maybe we can meet up again later, or tomorrow?"

We exchange numbers and part ways. I immediately text Roxy to see where she is, but I get no response. Then I try Casey. Ten minutes later and still nothing, so I conclude that they're either at Artist Alley or one of the underground panel rooms, since cell reception is notoriously bad at both of those locales.

It takes me almost half an hour to find them, but finally, I spot Devin's perfectly coiffed hair atop his tall figure. And sure enough, Roxana is with him. Though I am relieved to see that Casey is too. Roxana is waiting in line for another artist, and Devin is flipping through her Althena sketchbook.

"This is awesome," Devin is saying. "It's so clever to have one book dedicated to one character like this."

"Thanks!" Roxana responds. "I have some really amazing ones in there. Oh, that's one of my faves you just passed, actually."

I alert them all to my presence, and they say hello before continuing their conversation.

Fine, I self–pep talk as I watch Devin point out some technical detail about one of Roxana's favorite sketches. *But none of this will matter once I get the Zinc page.*

"So." I turn to Casey quietly. "Do we have a deal?"

Casey sighs. "I've been thinking about this a lot. . . ." Of course he has. He's Casey Zucker. The man is one big walking brain. "And . . . okay, yes. But just so I have a totally clear conscience . . . are you sure about this, man? It's a lot of money."

"I'm sure," I say gleefully, and hold out my hand for a high five.

He eyes it suspiciously but doesn't bring his own hand up. "Fine. Then tell me who's ranked number one."

"Felicia," I say without hesitation, because I know Casey is a man of honor and wouldn't renege on the deal now.

"Goddamn it!" he immediately responds before looking back up at my hanging five in exasperation. "I should have guessed that" is his next remark. And then, "Why does she have to be so perfect? Seriously, how can I possibly exploit a weak spot in *her*?"

He's right, of course. "I'll help you figure it out," I promise, though I also currently have no brilliant ideas on that front either. He sighs but finally bestows on me a weak high five.

As one of Roxana's favorite fictional detectives would say, the game is afoot!

I get a ping on my phone and find a text from Amelia.

Dude. You must look at the trending topics on Twitter right now.

I open the app and scroll down the list of trending topics. I stop when I see #InigoMontoyaSmackdown.

Must be a coincidence, I think. *It couldn't be . . .*

But when I click on the topic, a series of tweets come up, most of them retweeting a video.

A video starring a tall, lanky redheaded kid screaming a *Princess Bride* line at one scary-looking dude right in the middle of NYCC.

Chapter 17
WHAT'S HAIR GOT TO DO WITH IT?

"AGAIN. WE HAVE TO WATCH IT AGAIN," ROXANA SAYS. THEY'RE CROWDED around my phone, replaying the now apparently viral video.

I groan. "How many times do you need to relive my humiliation?"

"Humiliation?" Roxana says to me, blinking. "This is awesome."

"Really, dude. This is amazing," Devin confirms.

"You, like, saved the day," Roxy continues. "At *Comic Con*. If only you were wearing a cape."

I offer her a half-smile. "Charlie Noth doesn't do capes." In truth, I don't really know how to feel about the video. I mean, I am a little embarrassed, and the attention is bewildering. But it's also sort of cool. And most of the tweets and comments on the video are about how great it is, not what a dork I am (though, of course, there is some of that, too. This is the Internet, after all).

Casey, of course, wants to know the logistics of how I came up with that line. The video is too far away to make out the guy's scars-and-goatee combo, so I have to explain how my mind seemed to automatically project the *Princess Bride* villain onto him.

"A study in visual association," Casey concludes.

"Oh, hey. Here. Do you want this?" I take the pixel heart necklace out of my pocket and present it to Roxana—nonchalantly, as if it hasn't been burning a hole as soon as the booth girl told me it was for "my girl." "Spoils of my victory," I add.

Roxana takes a look into my palm. "Oh, wow. That is so cool," she says as she fingers the three hearts sitting next to each other on the bronze chain.

I gently push my hand in her direction, nudging her to take it. "It's yours."

"You sure?" she asks.

I smile at her. "I mean, I know it matches my hair and all, but I'm thinking you'll probably get more use out of it." I'm making jokes to mask the fact that my own heart is beating faster. After all, presenting the girl you secretly love with jewelry—even plastic jewelry—is no everyday occurrence.

"Well, thanks! This is awesome." She immediately clasps the chain around her neck, and I know I'm beaming at it, feeling like the happiness of seeing Roxy wear the literal hearts I just gave her might actually have the magic power to fill that last heart container right up. My pulse almost drowns out Casey as he tells us he needs to go, to keep to his schedule.

Eventually, I calm down enough to remember that Roxana and I have a Breaking into Comics panel at three o'clock and, as a bonus, I signed us up for a special critique by the duo leading it: Morgan Donnelly and Brandon Park, who also happen to be two of our creative team idols.

I give her a heads-up on this around two thirty.

"Awesome!" is her first reaction, before she gets nervous about the critique. "Wait, what pages did you bring for them to see?"

Since I was originally planning the whole day as a surprise, I haven't told her about this part either, but I think I know Roxana well enough to be able to pick out the pages from *Misfits of Mage High* that show off both her best work and mine.

She looks at the five pages I chose and flips through her work, stopping a couple of times at a panel that shows Master Vollux transforming into a sloth. "Do you think the shading"—I sense she's about to look up at me, and I get prepared to tell her how awesome I think it is, but she turns to Devin to finish her question—"on this panel looks right?"

He tilts his head to examine it, while I simply grit my teeth to keep from popping a vein. It takes him what I think is an insultingly long time to finally say, "Definitely. I think this is pretty perfect work, Roxana."

Roxana grins at him and then turns to give me the tail end of the same smile. "Okay! Let's do this."

Needless to say, my mood is nowhere near as buoyant as before, as I realize Devin is, of course, tagging along with us and that he has, somehow, managed to mooch off some of the glory for this plan of mine. It's only then that I start to wonder if he doesn't have some sort of actual superpower: like the ability to charm the pants off impressionable girls who have a nerd streak.

We're pretty early to the panel and manage to snag good seats near the front. Devin and Roxana chitchat some more while I continue to silently brood, but as soon as the panel starts, we all give our undivided attention to Morgan, the writer, and Brandon, the artist, as they talk about the business end of getting a comic series published. They go over everything from polishing up a spec pilot issue to querying agents or publishers to setting up a website for yourself, and even some marketing tactics. They have a short Q&A session too, but the two of us are hurriedly jotting down notes and don't get to be among the three fans who ask them anything.

At the end, Morgan announces that if we are one of the thirty people who signed up for a free critique, we can come up and hand in our work now. The online sign-up was on a first-come, first-served basis, and I can't help but smile privately to myself as I see the jealous looks in some of the audience members' eyes while Roxana and I get in line.

"I'll wait for you guys by the door," Devin needlessly promises, though

I'm relieved that he's not going to tag along to the critique, too.

Roxana and I are somewhere near the middle of the line when she insists on taking one more look at the pages.

"It's our best work, Roxy," I say soothingly. "You know it is."

She nods. "I know . . . it's just . . . maybe I could have done this differently." She points to an expository panel showing the moonlit silhouette of the school. It's simple and beautiful. "Is it clichéd?" she asks.

"I think it's great, but, you know, the point of the critique is to get an expert's take on your work. So we can both keep improving," I say gently.

She shakes her head and laughs. Before closing the folder, she says, "You're right. Of course."

When we finally get to the front of the line, Morgan and Brandon shake our hands as we gush to them about how much we admire their work.

"Thanks, guys," Morgan says. "And could you give me the title of this, whether it's part of a series, and a two-line synopsis?"

"Yes," I say, having rehearsed this part since I read the instructions for the critique. "This is part of our series *The Misfits of Mage High*, about a group of student mages who seem to each be extra gifted with certain small powers but are remedial in general knowledge. Hilarity and hijinks ensue."

Morgan smiles. "Sounds great." He jots a note down in an appointment book along with our names and asks us if 12:45 tomorrow is still a good time for us to come back for the critique itself. "Brandon and I will spend some time with the work overnight and then we'll have fifteen minutes tomorrow to discuss. Sound good?"

"Sounds excellent," Roxana says, and we leave the table feeling pretty exhilarated at the thought that Donnelly and Park will actually be reading and discussing *our* work.

"There's a panel on *Parallel Moon* next," I say hastily before we reach Devin and he can derail the plan I originally had for us. *Parallel Moon* is a new sci-fi show that Roxy and I have recently gotten into.

"Cool," Roxana replies. "Who's going to be there?"

I name the three main actors and the showrunner.

"Let's do it," she says, and then makes a beeline for Devin, who's been waiting for us at the side of the room. She of course immediately divulges our plan.

"Love that show," Devin says. Offfff course he does. I'm starting to suspect he's making at least some of these interests up just to impress Roxy.

But then he chimes in with "The last episode was really great, wasn't it? Especially the subplot with Marina and the vortex. I feel like that's going to come back later."

Damn it. Fine, he's a perfect, beautiful, British nerd. And I am totally screwed.

The panel is interesting enough, but somewhere in the middle my mind starts to wander. The John Hughes panel is next, and even though I've decided to put off my confession to Roxana until tomorrow—when I will hopefully have the Zinc page in hand—I still feel antsy. What if the perfect moment happens to arise today, after we've seen the panel and the movie? What if she gives me the perfect opening? I'm going to have to take it, right?

As applause signals the end of the panel, I pop up out of my chair, take Roxana's hand, and pull her up too. She laughs, startled. "Whoa! What's the rush?" she asks.

"The John Hughes panel is next," I say, and I'm pretty sure my voice squeaks. I clear my throat.

She grins. "So excited," she says, but then turns to Devin to comment on something we just heard about the next few episodes of *Parallel Moon*.

I frown. She's claiming to be excited, but I was expecting more of a reaction from her. Did I somehow overestimate how much she'd be into this, or is she playing it cool because of Devin? Like she wants to appear extra-sophisticated in front of him or something? If so, that's completely crazy, because she's about to go see some of her favorite actors talk about one of her favorite movies.

We exit the conference room and only have to go a few doors down to enter our next one. The John Hughes panel room has a medium-sized line in front of it, but we eventually get in and grab seats somewhere in the middle. Again, I feel nervous. But Roxana is at least now bouncing in her seat a little.

"Wow. I can't believe this is really happening," she whispers to me. I smile, thinking that's more like my girl. "I kinda feel like your mom is here with us too. Is that weird?"

I laugh and shake my head. "No. I feel like my mom would definitely be cool enough to haunt NYCC, especially for this."

A few seconds later, a moderator gets on the microphone at the front of the room and the crowd hushes. I recognize him, actually. He's a film critic for *Entertainment Weekly* and I think my mom knew him. In fact, I think he's acknowledged in one of her books. He speaks a little bit about John Hughes, explains the basic plot of *Pretty in Pink*—about a girl from the wrong side of the tracks who falls in love with a rich boy at school and the complications that ensue—and then introduces the panel. Out come the film's three big stars: Molly Ringwald, who plays the main girl, Andie; Andrew McCarthy, who plays the rich boy, Blane; and Jon Cryer, who plays Andie's geeky friend Duckie, who is also madly in love with her. They are followed by Anthony Michael Hall, who is not actually in *Pretty in Pink* but is an actor John Hughes cast a lot—often to play the nerdy character role—and director Howard Deutch, who helmed *Pretty in Pink*.

Everyone applauds thunderously and then immediately gets quiet to hear what the panelists have to say.

The moderator first asks them all to reflect on their work with John Hughes and what they think it is that makes his work endure. Molly Ringwald, who starred in three of his most famous movies, talks about how he really seemed to understand teenagers and treat them like fully formed characters instead of caricatures. Jon Cryer talks about how much heart Hughes's films have, while Anthony Michael Hall talks about how genuinely funny a lot of them are.

They get asked about being teen idols in the 1980s, and all of them speak about how different it was back then from the way it is today with the advent of social media and the concept of "being on" 24/7. Andrew McCarthy tells a funny story about posing for *Teen Beat* in the pre-Internet days when you didn't realize that something like that could live forever and come back to haunt you.

"I want to talk about the ending of *Pretty in Pink*," the moderator says then. "So the ending we all know and love, with Andie and Blane in the parking lot at prom . . ." He presses a button and a still from the film appears on the screen behind him. Sure enough, it's Molly Ringwald and Andrew McCarthy standing in a parking lot about to kiss. "That was not the original ending as written. Correct?"

"That's right," Jon Cryer says. "Because originally, I got the girl! Andie was supposed to end up with Duckie."

"Right," the moderator says. "Andie was supposed to end up with Duckie. The best friend who saw her and loved her for who she was right from the beginning. But I believe it was one of you who actually fought to get this ending changed." He looks piercingly at the panel, and Molly Ringwald raises her hand.

"Guilty as charged," she says.

"So now I want you to explain to this entire crowd of nerds," the moderator says to a huge burst of laughter, "why you didn't want Andie to end up with the geeky best friend."

Molly laughs too. "Oh, God! Are you turning them all against me?"

She twists around and looks up at the still of Blane and Andie. "You know, Andie and Duckie's relationship was so special. I truly believe they remained best friends for life. But if this had happened"—she indicates the imminent kiss behind her—"I think it would have ruined everything between them. And today, thirty years later, they wouldn't be friends. They wouldn't be in each other's lives. You know?"

I stiffen in my seat.

"What a bunch of bullshit," Jon Cryer says jokingly, and everyone laughs again. "I'm kidding. I'm just bitter because, again, I was *supposed to get the girl*. And then Andrew comes along with his perfect hair and his kitchen-appliance name . . ."

"Your hair was pretty spectacular too in this film, buddy," Andrew butts in.

The moderator clicks another button and we get a classic picture of Jon Cryer as Duckie with his pompadour, yellow cuffed-up blazer, and white snakeskin shoes. Jon looks up at it. "That's true. That was great hair." He turns to Molly. "Why didn't you want that guy, again?" he teases.

Molly puts her head in her hands. "I don't know. Oh, man, should I just admit I was wrong? Andie and Duckie should have ended up together?"

A cheer goes up from the crowd, and I'm not ashamed to say that my voice is among them.

Howard Deutch starts talking then. "Really, though, I think Molly's instincts were spot-on," he says. "We tested out the original ending where she ends up with Duckie, and it tested horribly. In fact, that scene that you just had up there was a reshoot that was done after the test screenings. And Andrew's great head of hair is actually a wig."

The moderator brings the original photo back up.

"Yes, which I think you can totally tell," Andrew says, laughing. "I had already shaved my head for a different movie role. Man, that thing was itchy."

"It changed the message of the movie in a positive way, I think," Howard goes on. "That two people from the opposite side of the tracks can belong together. Also, I think the chemistry was there between Molly and Andrew. Whereas, like Molly said, the chemistry between Molly and Jon was such a great friendship."

"All joking aside," Jon Cryer cuts in, "I do think all that is true."

They move on, to the topic of costuming and then to music, but I can't help lingering behind. They all think that's true? That a great friendship can't really turn into something more? That everything would get ruined? Was Duckie really too much of a geek for Andie? And is it really all about a great head of hair? I catch Devin's artfully styled locks from the corner of my eye, and I stew.

The panel ends with a Q&A session, and as per usual, most of the people who sprint their way to the mic have inane minutiae to hash out. One insists on pointing out all the continuity errors in the film (the moderator stops him at the third one). One asks how hard it was to pretend that Andie was such a great seamstress when her last outfit, the titular pretty in pink number in fact, was such a disaster. One simply asks if he can get his white snakeskin shoes autographed by the panel.

When the panel ends, there is more applause and hoots and hollers. I look over and see that Roxana is smiling from ear to ear. She beams that smile over in my direction and I can't help but return it to her. Honestly, I shouldn't read too much into what some fictional characters from thirty years ago did, right? This is my life, my story.

"The *Pretty in Pink* screening starts in half an hour," I say, and Roxy nods.

"Hey." Devin leans over, his phone clutched in his hand. "Instead of the movie, do you want to do something else?"

"Like what?" Roxana asks.

Yeah, like what, I think, gritting my teeth.

"My cousin who I'm staying with, he owns a karaoke bar around here. He says to come and bring friends tonight. He can get us in," Devin says, waving his phone around. "Especially if we get there earlier, like around six, before it gets too crowded."

Roxy seriously looks like she's mulling this over, which is absolutely ridiculous. "Well, I have to be on the nine p.m. train home, but . . ." She rubs her hand against the back of her hair. "Sure, why not?"

"What?" I voice that one objection out loud. "Are you serious? But *Pretty in Pink* . . . it's one of your favorite movies."

"I know, Graham, but that means I've seen it a hundred times. Besides, the panel was the special part, anyway." She nods toward the empty stage.

"Come on, man. It'll be fun!" Devin says as he and Roxana get up to leave the room. "And invite Casey or whomever else you want! We can fit up to ten people in one of the rooms."

I follow in their wake, stunned. So now we're going to do karaoke? What the eff?

In a daze, I text Casey. **Ummm . . . So Devin can apparently get us into a karaoke bar his cousin owns and Roxy wants to do that instead of the movie. You're invited too, Devin says.**

The bubble on my phone pops up, indicating that Casey got the text and is writing me back. But it stays as ellipses for a long time, which means that Casey is either typing something epic or really trying to piece together what to say about this mindfuck of a new development.

Finally, I get a shortish response back that indicates the latter. **Don't want to leave the convention. But . . . do you need me there or something?**

Need him? Of course not! *I'm not that close to an emotional break-down,* I think stubbornly. But then immediately feel bad. Poor Case. It must have taken all of his social skills to realize I might need backup with this one.

Nope, it's fine. Have fun at NYCC. Also pray for some miracle/accident that stops this from happening . . .

Chapter 18
WHAT'S THE OPPOSITE OF A REDEMPTION SONG?

THERE IS NO MIRACLE/ACCIDENT.

We're walking several avenues over, past Penn Station, and are about to enter a building that has the words SING OUT! emblazoned in neon across it. I cannot understand what has happened to my perfectly planned-out day.

"There he is!" another British voice rings out, and a shorter guy with dirty-blond hair and sporting a few tattoos holds the door open for us. He pats Devin on the back as he passes. "Come in, come in," he says with a smile to me and Roxana. "We'll do introductions inside, yeah?" He then turns to the large bouncer occupying 125 percent of a stool by the door. "They're with me."

The bouncer looks us over and grunts unhappily. "But you're not serving them drinks, Ryan. Right?"

"Of course not! Just the singing. Promise." He flashes another of what I'm now starting to suspect is a family-inherited prizewinning grin, and then he turns back to us where we're standing by the corner of the entrance. Even though it's barely 6 p.m., a girl is in the middle of the front room wailing "Wrecking Ball" with gusto. There are people sitting at the bar, flipping through thick books.

"We have a private room. This way," Ryan says, and leads us down a narrow hallway lit with purple lights to a door with the number nine on it.

We enter a small room with low leather benches set up along the sides. The place is dark, but outfitted with spinning red and green disco lights that are playing across the walls. It kind of looks like a Christmas rave. A couple of microphones and tambourines sit on a table in the center, along with more of the thick books I saw outside. A smiling blond girl is also waiting for us. She gets up as soon as we walk in and says hi.

"Right, now is a perfect time for introductions, I expect." Ryan introduces himself and his girlfriend, Elise. Devin takes over, introducing me and Roxana.

"Your first time at karaoke?" Ryan asks.

"Um, yes," I say, and barely manage to stop myself from adding that I am sixteen, so of course, dumbass.

"It's pretty simple," Ryan continues. "These books are divided alphabetically by song, and this one is divided by artist. Some of the newer songs are in the back. You just find your song, punch in its six-digit code on the remote"—he brandishes the small remote control that was sitting on the table—"and press Enter. And you can just enter songs whenever you want. The machine will queue them up in order."

"Sounds awesome, thanks!" Roxana says, and I just nod. I, obviously, have no intention of actually singing.

"Do you guys want to go first?" Ryan asks us, and we both shake our heads emphatically, Roxana with a nervous laugh.

"Then we'll get the party started, shall we, E?" Ryan turns to his girlfriend, who nods. "A classic?"

She grabs the remote and doesn't even look up a number in the book to punch it in. "Don't Go Breaking My Heart" comes up, and the two stand on opposite sides of the room, brandishing mics and ready to sing.

I don't know what I expected, maybe wannabe *The Voice* contestants or something, just based on how much they seem like karaoke pros, but that's not what happens. Both Ryan and Elise are clearly tone-deaf, and it's hard to tell which one is worse. But what they lack in talent, they make up for in enthusiasm, singing each word with dramatic emphasis and dancing around in choreographed moves. I hate to admit it, but it's kind of delightful in a thoroughly silly way. Devin and Roxana applaud thunderously when they're done, and even I have a stupid grin on my face.

"Who's next?" Ryan asks, eyeing me and Roxy. We both still shake our heads. "All right, Devin, ol' boy. Time to make our friends feel a little more comfortable. You think I'm bad, wait until you hear this guy."

"Okay, hold on. I think I'm going to try a new song." Devin gets a mischievous gleam in his eye as he flips through the song book and then punches in some numbers. The title flashes across the screen before the song begins. "Roxanne" by the Police.

As soon as the song begins with the title word, Devin gets on his knees in front of Roxana and sings it to her. She giggles.

And I watch incredulously as he serenades her with the whole song. I cannot believe this. Not only because Ryan is right and Devin is singing in at least three different keys, but "Roxanne"? Seriously? It's a song about a prostitute!

And just as I'm thinking Roxy has got to be so offended by this, I look over at her and realize that her eyes have turned into puddles. She looks like a manga girl.

Oh my God. What is happening?

Time seems to go by both agonizingly slowly, like when Devin finally convinces Roxana to duet with him on a song from *Grease,* and sometimes bizarrely fast, like whenever Ryan or Elise goes up and I can't help but be entertained by their antics. I glance at my watch every single minute that passes between 7:02 p.m. and 7:23 p.m. But then, the next time I look, it's almost 8 p.m.

I still haven't sung, despite repeated cajoling from all the members of our little group. Seriously, that's the last thing I need today.

Once Elise and Roxana are finished screaming out some Spice Girls number together, my watch triumphantly says what I've been beseeching it to all night. It's 8:30. Our train leaves in twenty minutes. I gleefully tell Roxy this. "We should go, and we probably need to book it to Penn Station to make it on time," I add for emphasis.

She looks at me, and her hand goes to the back of her head. Then, with a triumphant gleam in her eye, she takes out her phone and starts texting something. A minute later, the phone buzzes back, and she smiles at it.

"Excuse me one minute," she says as she takes her phone and leaves the room.

No one else seems to pay her departure much mind. Elise is singing, and both Ryan and Devin seem preoccupied with picking out their next song to butcher. But I, of course, wonder where the heck she's going.

I leave the room too, and glance down the purple-lit hallway. No sign of her. I guess she could have gone to the bathroom? But then what was that text about?

I follow the hallway anyway, keeping an eye out for her. I scan the front room when I get there. It's gotten more crowded, but almost everyone there is staring raptly at the guy at the mic, who is rapping an Eminem song with some serious skills. Unfortunately, none of this captive audience is my best friend.

She didn't take her coat with her, so it's stupid to probably even do this, but . . . just in case, I open the front door and peek outside.

And there she is. Shivering slightly and talking on her phone. She has one hand on her right ear to block out the city noise, but I hear her end of the conversation perfectly. "So I'm just going to stay at Felicia's for a little while after I get back from Comic Con. There's a math test on Monday we're both a little nervous about. Thought we'd study for it one last time together." She pauses while she listens to the other end. "Midnight," she finally says. "I definitely won't be home later than that. Okay, Baba. See you soon."

She presses End on her phone, and when she sees me standing there, she gives me a victorious grin.

"Lying again?" I say, and it sounds accusatory, even to my own ears. But the truth is, I'm not impressed.

She snorts. "Geez. Calm down, *Officer*." I'm still scowling, so she continues in an equally accusatory tone. "It was your idea yesterday, remember? The whole 'Cut school and fool your parents, Roxy' bit?"

But it's not my idea today. And the thing is, I'm not really sure it's entirely Roxana's idea either. This new sorta rebellious Roxy, making plans on a whim and singing duets and lying to her parents again, I don't think I quite know her. And I definitely can't help but feel that Devin is the one bringing all this out.

Roxana goes to reenter the karaoke bar, but we get stopped by the bouncer. *Awesome,* I think. *We won't be able to get in and that'll be the end of that.*

Unfortunately, it's the same bouncer as before, and as soon as Roxy mentions Ryan's name, he remembers us and ushers us back in. So much for that plan.

When we get back to the room, there's a new addition: a pitcher of beer, along with some fresh cups. "Don't tell," Ryan says with a wink. He pours a cup for Roxana and hands it to her.

She stares at it for a moment, then takes a sip. She immediately makes a face at the taste.

"What? It's not that bad!" Devin says. "We sprang for only the moderately cheap stuff."

Roxana smiles and takes another small sip. She reflexively makes another face. But I notice she doesn't put the drink down.

"Okay, so is it this beer in particular or beer in general? 'Cause maybe we can get something else?" Devin asks in concern. As if that's what he should be worried about: that Roxana doesn't like the taste of beer, not that her personality seems to have done a complete 180 in the last twenty-four hours. Because I know for a fact that she's never had a drink before.

"I'm not much of a drinker," she lies again.

"Oh," Devin says, and then, after a moment, slaps his forehead. "Right. I forgot. Drinking's kinda hard here when you're underage, right? I'm actually legal drinking age in the UK, but it's sorta not as big of a deal there. You obviously don't really have to drink that."

But Roxana smiles and takes another sip. "Nah, it's okay. It's always good to try something new, right?"

It's official. I hate this. But I can't say anything now, not after she already called me out for policing her.

"Graham?" Ryan is holding out a full cup of beer for me now. I stare at the amber liquid filling the small plastic cup. At this point, why the hell not? I take it.

It's definitely not tasty. But I finish it quicker than Roxana finishes hers. And when Ryan asks if I want another one, I acquiesce. The third one, I even pour for myself.

At one point, Elise is shoving the karaoke book in my hands. "Come on, Graham. You have to sing at least one song. I promise, it's not that bad once you get up there. It's *fun*."

I'm really not that interested, but my defenses are weakened, so I take the book from her, if only to shut her up. I'm flipping through the pages when a title sticks out at me. It's called "Something on the Quiet" and it's by this kind of obscure British band called the Silver Bells that my dad listens to sometimes. It's an old song, from the sixties, with doo-wops and ooh-aahs in it. I immediately start humming it in my head, and then I get to the line at the end of the chorus. *"I'm in love with you."* And before I know it, I'm carelessly punching its numbers into the remote.

In the meantime, the four of them sing the songs they've already put in. At one point, Devin is touching Roxy's shorn hair, and it's making me feel ill. I pour myself another drink.

Then the opening notes of my song begin. Everyone looks around, wondering who put it in, and when I finally weakly raise my hand, Elise gives a squeal of delight and everyone else hoots and hollers, shouting my name in encouragement.

Elise hands me the mic and I stand up. If nothing else, it'll be a good private joke with myself, maybe even a way to relieve some tension. Roxana will never know that I'm singing the song to her. That I'm pouring my heart out to her.

"Can I tell you something on the quiet? Though maybe you already know." I sing the opening lyrics, instinctively looking at my best friend, the secret girl of my dreams. She's grinning at me.

"I'll whisper it soft and light. 'Cause sometimes words can ignite and explode," I continue.

"Wow! You have a nice voice!" Elise shouts out in encouragement, and Roxana nods enthusiastically. The boys are still woo-hooing at key points.

But then I'm not even looking at the lyrics on the screen anymore. Just at Roxana as I sing the words. It's such a simple song, and a song that's a million years old. But it doesn't matter. It's everything I want to say.

> *"I don't want to sound an alarm.*
> *I don't want to cause any harm.*
> *We're friends to the end.*
> *That's truer than true.*

Chapter 19
I LEFT MY HEART ON THIRTY-SEVENTH STREET

THE SONG ENDS AND DEVIN, ELISE, AND RYAN ALL CHEER FOR ME. ROXANA simply stands up, grabs my hand, and leads me out the door. My heart is pounding in time to whatever pop song is blaring from the karaoke machine by the bar. The hallway's purple lights make everything doubly surreal: is this the walk to my execution or my salvation?

Roxana makes a beeline for the bar's front door, pulling me in her wake. But as soon as we get outside, she lets go of my hand, walks a bit down the street, puts her hands through her hair, and then finally turns to look at me.

"What . . . ," she starts, out of breath, "what was that?"

But I've been holding on
For far, far too long
To what's in my heart:
I'm in love with you."

And right then, as I say the words that made me punch in the numbers in the first place, something in Roxana's face changes. Her mouth turns into a little o as she stares at me. And that's when I realize: she knows.

I have finally just told—nay, sung to—my best friend that I love her.

I realize I have two choices. I could feign ignorance. "What was what?" I could ask. Pretend like I was doing nothing more than belting out a song. Because, obviously, this is not how I intended this to happen at all. Of every scenario I ever dreamt up—the realistic and the totally fantastical—singing a cheesy old song at karaoke was never in the picture.

But it doesn't matter now. It's out there and I can't take it back. So I man up and take the second option. I say it in my own words this time, the simplest words. "I love you, Roxana. I'm in love with you."

She's staring at me, frozen. Then she's shaking her head and looking down at the concrete. Then back up at me. Over and over again, her head just shaking. There are decades of silence.

Finally, she breaks it. "How? When?" she croaks out.

"I . . . how? What does that mean?"

"Just . . . when?"

"I mean, I guess for a long time now." I start out slowly, because even though I've rehearsed some version of this for months, I can't seem to conjure up those perfectly practiced words now. "But I realized it over the summer. It's like I woke up the morning after the hospital with your grandmother and I just knew. . . ." I look at her and her chalk-white face and her mouth that can't seem to stop making that little o, and suddenly, I'm a little exasperated. "Come on, Roxy. You can't tell me you didn't really know. That some small part of you . . ."

"I didn't!" she practically screams at me.

"So it just never even crossed your mind that you and I could be more than friends?" My voice is raised now too.

"Of course it crossed my mind!"

I startle in the middle of my breakdown. "Wait . . . it did?"

"Of course!" she says as she begins to pace, her hand frantically going through the back of her hair. "You're a guy, and we've grown up together. I'm sure we were hanging out around the time I realized that you can get crushes on boys, and that things can feel different than just between friends. And there were moments . . ." She's staring at her hands, and I have to wonder if she's thinking of that night at the hospital too—when they were clasped with mine. I wait, wanting her to go on, but she doesn't, instead just pacing back and forth in silence and making an absolute mess of her hair. I watch the pixel heart necklace swing back and forth agitatedly and I can't help but stare at the last heart—the one that's half full. Or, depending on your perspective, I suppose, the one that's half empty. Or, perhaps, simply broken.

When I feel like I can't stand the silence another second, I miserably provide the word I know she's looking for, thinking my stay of execution has gone on long enough. "But . . ."

After a few more interminable moments, she finally stops pacing right in front of me and looks up at me. "But . . . nothing ever happened. And I realized this is us. We're best friends. We do everything together. What about *Misfits*? What about how easy everything is? How could it possibly be worth it to mess that up?"

I think my own heart has dropped somewhere well below my body, down into the concrete. Maybe even it's riding a subway train now, far, far away from here. Because I get what she's saying. That I somehow missed the boat and now the thought of us together is literally not worth it to her. *I'm* not worth it to her.

I swallow hard, feeling it echo through my hollow limbs. "So . . . now what?" I mutter, but I'm talking to myself.

Except Roxana doesn't get that. "Exactly. Now what, Graham?" She throws her hands up in the air. She sounds pissed, and suddenly that makes me angry. I just poured my heart out to her. She totally rejected me. And now she's *mad at me?*

We glare at each other for a few seconds more, and then I look at my watch. "Well, it's ten thirty," I say, my voice magically steady as if it's an entity apart from everything churning inside me. "We have to catch a train soon."

"Right," she says as she yanks the door of the bar open. The bouncer doesn't even stop us this time as we march back to the room.

When we get in there, Devin starts to ask if everything is all right, but Roxana cuts him off. "We have to catch our train now," she says with a fake smile and a syrupy-sweet voice that sounds more off than the Mariah Carey song Ryan is currently interpreting.

I just stand by the door as they say their good-byes and mutter mine on cue. I vaguely realize that Devin is making plans to see Roxana again tomorrow at NYCC, but I barely hear it. Everything suddenly looks and sounds as if it's underwater.

When we leave the bar for the final time, Roxana walks briskly out in front of me, and I make no attempt to catch up to her, just follow her familiar gait all the way to Penn Station. My head is down, but the streetlamps paint her shadow across my path. If I had all my writerly wits about me, I'm sure I could make it into a metaphor for something. But right now, whatever primal emotional preservation method courses through my body kicks in and I feel numb to my core. Or maybe it's the beer. I'm thinking I wouldn't mind if this lasted awhile, like maybe for a few years, until I can be positive I'll be totally over this abject rejection.

Our train is at the platform when we arrive at the station. We go down the stairs to catch it, and that's the only time Roxana says anything to me. "I texted Felicia, and her brother can come pick us up."

I give a small nod.

She stops walking then and lets me get on the train first. I immediately realize it's so that I can choose a seat and she can choose one somewhere down the car.

That's fine. As soon as I sit down, I search through my backpack and put my headphones on. But scrolling through my phone, I realize there's no music I want to listen to. Music will probably unleash all the emotions that are being strangely kept at bay, and I can't afford to throw a gift like that away.

I keep the headphones on anyway. They're a decent pair, and they cancel out most of the noises of the train. It's not that crowded because it's too early for most of the rowdy drunk crowd to be heading home after a Saturday night out, but there are still some conversations happening in the car that I'd prefer not to hear: a loved-up couple two rows behind me, some girl telling her friend about the amazing second date she just had.

With the headphones on, I mostly just feel the rumble of the train. And then I close my eyes, and I can almost pretend to be on any train, going anywhere. I can be in a 1920s detective novel or a sci-fi intergalactic flight. I can be anyone, too. Anyone except Graham Posner on this night in October. That sounds like a step up to me.

"The skies swallowed her up and the stars glittered coldly on—feeling nothing for one shattered heart on one insignificant planet," Charlie says at the end. **"They shine and shine but all is dim."**

No. For once, I don't want to be Charlie Noth, either. Even though I feel closer to understanding his feelings than I ever have before.

With determination, I manage to keep my mind pretty clear as we rumble back to Huntington. Anytime anything even remotely unpleasant threatens to surface, I just pop it like a bubble. Or better yet, punch it like in an old episode of Adam West's *Batman*. Rox—POW! Karao—BAM! Even Robert Zi—gets KABOOMed.

I'm not asleep exactly when we finally arrive, but it takes me a while to realize the train has stopped. When I open my eyes, my car is almost empty and Roxana is nowhere in sight. I grab my backpack and amble out.

She's waiting for me outside. She points out Emile's car in the parking lot, and I follow her to it.

Felicia is sitting in the passenger seat, so Roxana and I open opposite doors in the back and slide in.

"Hi, guys!" Felicia says.

"Hi," Roxana immediately responds, extra loudly; maybe she thinks she can pass that off as her usual chirpiness. "Thanks so much for picking us up! I owe you one, Emile."

"Yes, thank you," I echo in hollow tones.

"No problem," Emile says as he pulls out of the parking lot.

"So . . . how was it today?" Felicia asks brightly.

"Fine," Roxana says stiffly, and I just nod. Silence permeates the car.

"Just . . . fine?" Felicia asks, and her sharp eyes glance at us in the rearview mirror.

"Well, you know. It was great," Roxana says, again substituting volume for enthusiasm. "The usual nerd stuff we love. We don't want to bore you."

At this point, Felicia has turned back to look Roxana in the face and gets met with a toothy smile. Then Felicia turns to me, and I will my mouth to turn up too.

She looks back and forth between us for a second longer and then sneaks a glance at her brother before finally turning around in her seat, like she's desperate to find out what's happening but knows better than to ask in front of him.

"Sounds awesome," she finally says. "But you guys sound exhausted."

"Yes, definitely," Roxana says, her voice now flooded with relief.

Ten minutes later, Emile pulls into my driveway. I thank him and Felicia again before scrambling out of the car and up to my front door, my keys already in hand. I cannot get away from that Toyota Prius and its current inhabitants fast enough.

Chapter 20
FALLOUT

THE NUMBNESS STICKS WITH ME AS I METHODICALLY PREPARE FOR BED, AND I'm starting to think I'll fall asleep that way. But then, from the corner of my eye, I glimpse something on my wall: a few of the *Misfits of Mage High* panels that I love the most and have tacked up there. Suddenly, one moment comes back like a pinprick to a balloon and jolts all my nerves awake—what Roxy said about *Misfits*.

She didn't want anything to change, and now everything has. How will we ever write together again? Or talk? Or do anything without it being supremely awkward? Have I destroyed everything I built up over the past eight years in one fell swoop?

A tear escapes my eye. I hastily wipe it away and shut my eyes tight so that no more tears can come. It takes me a very long time to fall asleep.

After only a couple of fitful hours of rest, I wake up the next day with a pounding headache and dry, red eyes. I only remember halfway through dressing that I'm probably experiencing something of a hangover. Coupled with a shattered heart, of course. Terrific.

The original plan was for Roxana's mom to drive Samira, Roxy, and me to the train station this morning, but I immediately self-veto this. Instead, I go downstairs and ask my dad if he can give me a ride. He agrees, and I send Roxana a quick text that takes me way too long to compose, since I want to come across as casual and non-brokenhearted as possible. **No need for a ride today. My dad will drop me off** is what I finally settle for.

K, she texts back after five minutes. Which I desperately attempt (and mostly fail) not to read anything into.

On the drive over, my dad asks what's going on at the con today and I mumble something about panels because, honestly, I don't even remember what I had originally planned for the day.

"Sounds fun. Maybe next year, I can come with you guys on one of the weekend days," he says.

"Yeah. Maybe." Next year. That seems impossible right now. That the minutes, hours, and days will tick away enough for us to be at New York Comic Con again one whole year later. How can I possibly occupy

that time without my best friend and my writing partner? How excru-
ciating will all those moments be?

I'm absentmindedly staring at my dad's hands on the steering wheel,
and the shiny gold band on his left hand twinkles at me. Out of nowhere
a thought hits me. I've asked my dad to recall the day he met my mom
hundreds of times. In the beginning, it was about them, their story. But
later on, I wanted to hear it because it gave me hope as an awkward
nerd myself. That my dad got up the nerve to approach a pretty girl
and strike up a conversation, even if the impetus for it was misguided.

But now I realize . . . I don't know much about the rest. How did
they keep talking? How did he ever tell her he loved her? Eventually
propose to her?

There's only one person I can ask this of now. I might as well.

"Dad?"

"Hmmm?"

"When did you tell Mom you loved her?"

He quickly glances at me then, surprised enough by the question to
momentarily take his eyes off the road. But then he bursts out laughing.
"On our third date," he confesses. "I was an idiot. It was a miracle she
didn't bolt out of the restaurant and never come back."

I smile weakly and take that in before I think of a follow-up question. "And did you actually love her by the third date?"

"Of course!" he says. "But I should've played it at least a little bit
cooler, you know? Anyone less perfect for me probably never would

have stood for it." I see a sad, secret smile play on his lips.

"What about Lauren? When did you tell her?"

"Ah. Well, I was definitely older and wiser. And it was a different, more mature relationship. Plus, you know, I was still grieving for Evie for a long time, even when we first started dating. So it took a while. But I told her on our one-year anniversary, when we went to the Hamptons for a weekend. I planned the whole thing out that time."

I nod, thinking my situation sounds like a combination of the two. Planned out and thought about . . . but urgent and spontaneous, too.

"I love Lauren, too, you know," Dad says quietly, and I turn to him, slightly alarmed.

"I know," I assure him.

"There's a part of you that thinks it's not supposed to work out that way," Dad continues slowly, his eyes on the road. "That you get one great love and to try again with anyone else would be an abomination to that memory. I never thought I would have to find love again, obviously, when I married your mom. And after she was gone, I never thought I ever could . . . I never looked for it—" I'm alarmed to realize that he's sounding apologetic.

"Dad," I interrupt him. "I'm glad you have Lauren. I'm glad we both do." And it's true. She loves my dad, and she's always been good to me, even if she doesn't quite understand me. Maybe I didn't comprehend their relationship so well when I was nine, but now that I'm older— and now that I have an inkling of what love actually is—I do. I think

Lauren was the only way my dad was ever going to heal from losing my mom. Not get over it, precisely, but heal.

"Is there something that's brought this on?" my dad prods gently as we turn into the train station parking lot.

I sigh. "Something," I concede. "Maybe we can talk about it later."

He nods. "I'm here to listen whenever."

I smile at him. "Thanks. See you."

"Do you have a ride back?" he asks as I'm getting out of the car. Oh, man, a loaded question. Once again, Roxy's mom was supposed to pick us up.

"Um, not sure. Can I call you if I need?"

"You bet."

We say good-bye and my dad drives off. The train hasn't arrived, so I walk slowly to the empty platform, my eyes darting around like I'm stalking prey. No one else is here yet, but a few minutes later, Casey gets dropped off. And just as I'm about to say hello to him, a familiar burgundy sedan pulls up too, and Roxana and Samira pile out, and then, to my surprise, Felicia.

"I didn't know Felicia was coming today." Casey voices my thoughts.

"Me neither," I mutter. When the three girls come up to us, Casey asks Felicia about her surprise appearance and Felicia says she snagged a last-minute pass on eBay last night. "I had so much fun on Friday, I thought why not?" she says cheerily, but I notice she doesn't meet my eye. Of course, Roxana must have told her what happened, and she's here for moral support. Or maybe even to make sure I don't renew my declarations of affection or whatever.

The train pulls up and we find an available five-seater, three seats facing one way and two the other. The third seat is always a shorter one, with uncomfortable metal bars where the headrest would otherwise be. But after Roxana slides into the window and Samira slides in next to her, I take that one. This way I'm not facing Roxana and I'm one seat away from her too. It's the farthest we can get from each other while still pretending to be part of the same group.

On the way in, Samira chatters about how she's so excited about her first NYCC and, thankfully, fills up a lot of the silence. Felicia and Casey chime in, and even Roxy and I pick up cues here and there— whenever we're sure it can't be construed as us having a conversation with each other. At one point, when Samira is asking Roxana a complicated question about the logistics of the autograph line, I see Casey eyeing Felicia thoughtfully, and I vaguely wonder if he's going to bring the class ranking thing up today. And then I sort of wish my biggest problem right now was academic in nature too: study enough, strategize enough, and it's likely solvable. Completely the opposite of this tangled emotional turmoil that seems to have no logical solution.

It isn't too hard to let the others steer the conversation on the walk over to the Javits, either. Besides, it's cold and we're walking against the wind. It's like nature is on my side for once, making it harder to be chatty.

When we scan our badges and get inside, Devin is waiting for us by the door. It's funny because, after everything that's happened, I almost forgot about him. He calls out to Roxana, gets introduced to Samira, and says hello to everyone else.

"You doing all right?" he asks with a smile when he gets to me.

I'm suddenly furious. Whoa. Did Roxana actually tell this guy about my humiliation last night? "What the hell do you mean?" I spit out.

Devin looks bewildered. "Just whether you're hungov—"

"He's fine." Roxana cuts him off sharply and then turns around and glares at me. As if I was the one about to use the word *hungover* in front of her little sister.

"Yup. Completely fine," I respond, my voice as bitter as arsenic. "Thanks for clearing up my feelings for me, Roxana. You are terrifically talented at that."

Her mouth drops open a little, but her eyes turn into slits. I can perfectly read the question that's written in her angry stare: *Are we really going to do this here and now?*

No, we're not, I decide. "Excuse me, but I have a panel to get to," I say forcefully, and march past the group into the bowels of the convention center. I hear the squeak of sneakers start after me.

"Wait," Casey says when he catches up. "What panel?" He's gotten his spreadsheet schedule out and is frantically looking at it.

I sigh, irritated. "I don't know. There is no panel. Don't worry about it." I keep walking.

"What?" Casey asks, looking thoroughly confused but still following me anyway.

I grimace but keep up my pace, aimlessly wandering onto the show floor. Then I finally break my silence. "I accidentally told Roxy everything last night. It didn't . . . go well."

"Oh," Casey says, and it takes him a long time to think to say, "I'm sorry."

I wave his pity away, looking at the dozens of colorful booths surrounding us but not really seeing any of them. "Forget it. Look, *is* there some panel we can go to right now? Or something? Anything?"

Casey consults his spreadsheet again and says there's a Female Superheroes panel that he wants to check out in ten minutes because one of his favorite artists is on it. Also, female superheroes.

"Great," I say, and tell him to lead the way. We manage to get seats near the front. I play a game on my phone to pass the time while we wait, but even when the panel starts, I find it difficult to pay attention. I'm ferociously trying not to replay any part of last night, and then any part of the weekend, and then, inevitably, most parts of the last eight years of my life. And that's hard, especially when I can't even seem to focus on the unrelated discussion happening in front of me.

Then I realize that the best thing I can do to distract myself *is* to really listen to the panelists and get each of their respective opinions on female superheroes. I do want to hear about Wonder Woman and Storm and Captain Marvel. I want to hear *all* about them. . . .

But then we reach the end of the panel and Lacey Grotowski—who is a panelist—inevitably gets asked about being one of the few women in her field, and with a pang, Roxana's voice is in my ear. Just this summer, in fact, when we were eating dried sour cherries in her backyard and taking a break from a brainstorming session, we were discussing when we thought we'd achieve one of our biggest goals: the first time we'd be asked to be on a Comic Con panel.

"I'm going to be optimistic and say first year out of college," I said.

She looked at me. "Okay, let's put it out into the universe, then." She turned her face up into the cloudless sky. "Universe. Graham Posner and Roxana Afsari will get their first invitation to speak at a Comic Con before they're twenty-three." And I swear a bird chirped in response.

"Nice going, Snow White." I smiled at her.

"Oh, but there's one thing more, Universe," she continued, staring up. "No matter what else happens, I ask of you to ban one question forevermore from the Q&A section . . ."

Then she kept me waiting, and I knew she wanted me to try and guess. "'Where do you get your ideas?'"

"Nope." She shook her head.

"Calling you out on a nitpicky detail?"

"Nope."

"Okay, I give up."

She smiled and turned her head to the sky once more. "Please don't let anyone ask me what it's like to be one of the only women in my field."

"Is that because you're hoping by then you won't be one of the only women in your field?"

"Definitely," Roxana said. "Also, it's a stupid question. It's like me asking you: Graham, what's it like to be one of the few redheaded writers?"

And I saw her point.

As I see and hear Lacey calmly and gracefully answer the question now, I realize that it's something she must get all the time. And something none of the male artists sitting up there with her probably ever get.

Five minutes later, the panel is over, and of course, trying to focus on anything other than my worries hasn't worked at all. I'm truly at a loss as to how I can extricate my life and memories from Roxana.

As we get up to leave, my phone buzzes. It's a text from Felicia asking where I am. I ignore it.

"Where are you off to next?" I ask Casey, who, after consulting his spreadsheet, says there's a raffle for exclusive NYCC Christmas ornaments at the Hallmark booth. "Great," I respond, thinking maybe I can at least get my dad's birthday present early this year.

But then my phone buzzes again. **Samira's asking for you. She said she thought you also wanted to get a photo with Aaron Dunning?** Felicia writes.

I sigh. She's right; I promised I'd go with her to meet him.

I only take another moment before I text Felicia back. **Meet you near the autograph line.**

Because I know that no matter what's happened, I can't let Samira down. She's practically my little sister too.

There's another buzz, and I expect it to just be a confirmation text from Felicia, but it's something else entirely.

How's it going today, Inigo?

Amelia.

Despite everything, I manage a little smile. It feels like the first time I've been compelled to smile since last night.

Same ol' same ol', I respond. **Looking for Miracle Max. Seeking revenge.** An image of Devin's perfect face flashes through my mind at that last statement.

I'll keep an eye out for the man with 6 fingers, she writes back.

Please do.

Chapter 21
JUST LIKE FAN FIC

CASEY WALKS WITH ME TO THE AUTOGRAPH AND PHOTO OP SECTION AND helps me find Aaron Dunning's name—and subsequently Samira, Felicia, Roxana, and Devin. Roxana and Devin are deep in conversation about something, but Felicia waits with Samira until they see me approach. Sam gives me a wide grin and waves a piece of paper she's holding in her hand.

"Excited?" I ask her as I eye the paper and see it's a receipt for the photo op.

She nods, her eyes wide and bright.

"I'm going to go check out the ornaments, and then I have another panel to get to," Casey says.

"What is it?" Felicia asks.

"Oh. It's, um, Dothraki 101." Casey blinks a few times.

"Dothraki," Felicia starts. "That sounds kinda familiar."

"It's a language from *Game of Thrones*," I helpfully provide. "I think the guy who helped create it for the show is here. Right, Casey?"

Casey nods.

"Oh, cool. Mind if I come?" Felicia asks.

Casey blinks several more times and then nods again. If I didn't know any better, I'd say he's blushing.

"Where and when should we meet you guys?" Felicia turns to me.

"Um . . . how about in an hour? At the DC Comics display in the middle of the show floor?" There are a lot of movie props there, and I've been meaning to take a look. Specifically at some of the Tim Burton *Batman* stuff. Amelia's little argument from yesterday has stuck with me.

"You know where that is, right, Casey?" Felicia asks him.

Casey nods again and manages to mutter a "yeah" this time too.

"Great! See you guys then! Lead the way," Felicia says to Casey, and I see my mute and blinking best friend walk in a daze as the one and only Felicia Obayashi follows him. I give a small chuckle in spite of everything. Because I have no idea what's going on there, but it's kinda delightfully bizarre.

"We have that art panel, too, Roxana. Right?" I hear Devin's voice.

"Yeah . . ." Roxana hesitates. I casually glance over to see her looking at Samira.

"You guys can go," I say in their general direction, not really looking at them. "I'll hang with Sam. We can all meet at the DC display in an hour." But when I get only silence, I have to break my rule and glance at Roxana's face.

She's looking between me and Samira, like she's worried, and I feel a pang. What? Like I suddenly can't be trusted with her little sister anymore? Seriously?

I stare at her then, defiantly, until she looks away with the decency to at least appear a little embarrassed.

"Okay," she finally says, and the two of them disappear into the crowd, while Samira and I follow the sign for Aaron Dunning and get onto the back of his photo line. I notice that the line is mostly teen and preteen girls like Sam. But whatever.

"So, what's up?" she asks.

"Not much. What's up with you?"

She rolls her eyes. "No. I mean what's up with you and my sister?"

I smile down at her. "Nothing."

"That's bull," she says in what I recognize as her mother's no-nonsense voice. "You know it. I know it. So will you please tell me what's going on?"

My smile is faltering, and I'm not sure exactly what to say to her. It was foolish of me to think she wouldn't catch that lie—she's smart and observant so there's no way she didn't pick up on my tiff with Roxy this morning. I think on it a moment before settling for, "I said some stuff to her last night. And she didn't take it well. So now . . . I don't know. Things are weird."

"You mean, like, a fight?"

"Something like that," I agree. A fight sounds better than the truth.

Samira frowns. "Wow. I didn't know you guys had fights."

"We don't usually. But, you know . . . things change," I say vaguely.

She mulls this over for a second and then shrugs. "Well, it's okay. Just apologize. Or I'll talk to her and have her apologize to you. Whose fault is it, anyway?"

"Mine," I say at once, though I also immediately realize that's not entirely accurate. It's not like I purposefully fell in love with her. It just happened.

"Then apologize," Sam reiterates firmly. "You're sorry, aren't you?"

Am I sorry for loving Roxana? I feel like shit, and things may never be the same again. So I'm sorry for all that. But how can I be apologetic for caring about her like that? "I don't know," I finally say. "It's a little complicated, Sam. Hey, have you given any thought to a specific pose you want to do in this photo or anything?" I point over to the photo pickup place, where some of the images from the previous days are on display. There's a small section of Aaron Dunning ones, and a few of the people are striking the same iconic pose he did on the poster for *Pterodactyl II*.

I look back at Sam, but she's not looking at the photos. Instead, she's staring at me thoughtfully. "Listen, are you guys, like, secretly in love or something?"

"Me and Aaron Dunning?" I say, even as my heart sinks.

"No! You and Roxana."

"Um . . ." I can't think of any other response, but it seems to be all the encouragement Samira needs.

"I mean, it makes total sense." She starts out slowly. "You see it all the time on the fan fic forums, right? Two best friends, who then secretly fall in love. And then, of course, there will be some complications, because, obviously, there has to be conflict. . . ." Despite everything, I smile at that. It's one of the first things I ever taught her about writing a story, back before she was kind of a big deal on her forums in her own right. "But eventually, it all works out and they live happily ever after. So there you are," she says triumphantly. "We just have to get to the happily ever after part. If you're really in love, I mean. So are you?"

My eyes dart around as I try to figure out the right, least traumatic answer I can possibly give Roxana's little sister.

"Just tell me!" she demands.

"I . . . okay, yes. I love your sister." I give in. It's too hard to come up with anything else right now, with my screwy, addled brain getting all tangled up with my screwy, addled emotions.

"You're in love with her," Samira reiterates slowly.

"Yup," I confess miserably.

A slow grin starts spreading across her face, and I wonder if there's a sadistic side to her that I haven't quite noticed before. "That's sooooo sweet!" she finally says, and I realize that nope, she's just an eleven-year-old girl who reads and writes a lot of love stories.

"Well, not exactly, Sam," I say with a lopsided grin. "Thing is, she's not in love with me."

"She said that?" she asks incredulously.

I shrug. "Not in those exact words. But the gist of it."

"Okay. Can you tell me what happened. Exactly?" she asks, as if I'm her patient and she wants my symptoms.

I sigh. Guess I might as well at this point. So I tell her about karaoke, though I leave out the alcohol and the fact that Roxy lied to her parents about where she was. Just that I sang a stupid song, thinking I was being all stealthy, and, clearly, I wasn't. "And then she freaked out and asked me why I'd want things to change."

"Annnnd?"

"And that's it. We had an awkward train ride home. Another one this morning. And everything since has been just that: extremely awkward."

"But," Samira butts in, "she didn't say she didn't love you."

I stare at her. "I think it was pretty well implied."

She shakes her head. "No. Maybe you caught her off guard. Maybe she needs time to think."

I shake my head back at her, but luckily I'm saved from having to give a response because we've reached the front of the line and are now being ushered behind the black curtain, where Aaron Dunning is having photos taken. That's good, because I have no response.

Samira tells the girl who takes her receipt that she wants both of us to be in the photo. I ask her if she's sure and she says yes.

Aaron says hello to us and shakes our hands. He gives Samira a "How are you doing?" and a smile, which makes her blush furiously. Though not as much as when he puts his arm around her shoulder while they take the photo. I only notice this a few minutes later when we go to pick up the finished product. Samira looks about the same color as Aaron's artfully draped tomato-red scarf, but she doesn't even seem to notice. She looks so flushed and happy that I have to grin.

"When's your next big event?" I ask her.

"The fan fiction panel is at two," she replies. *Maybe I'll accompany her to that, too,* I think.

On our way to the DC display to meet the others, we pass by the Sun Auctions booth again. I look at my watch. The auction starts in a few hours.

As we come up to the glass case, I can't help staring at the small Zinc display, where, I swear, my page glows like it's a prop from *Indiana Jones*. All my plans, everything I so meticulously plotted to make happen—gone in a stupid instant. Alcohol sucks. I'm never drinking again.

I guess I've come to a full stop in front of the display, because that's where Felicia and Casey find us, and Casey immediately sees what I'm looking at.

"Do you think you're still going to buy it?" he asks, and I stare at the physical manifestation of my erstwhile hopes and dreams.

"I wish I could turn back time," I respond. *Like Rewinder,* I privately think. Only I would go back a whole day, not forty-five minutes. So like a matured Rewinder, then—one who is in full possession of her powers.

"What are you talking about?" Felicia asks lightly.

"Oh. Graham was going to buy that for Roxana," Casey blurts out in his usual blunt way, pointing at the page.

Both girls peer into the case. "Whoa!" Felicia says. "Five hundred dollars for a piece of paper?"

"No, it's five hundred dollars to start," Casey corrects. "It'll probably go for a few thousand at least."

Felicia steps closer, and I realize she's reading the pages. "Oh," she says quietly after a moment. "I see."

I know she doesn't know much about Althena, but I guess she gets the gist of what's going on between Althena and Noth there—especially considering she's probably written twenty-page analytical English papers about, like, Tolstoy. I hear a soft "Awwwww" escape from under Samira's breath and I realize she's read it now too.

Well, at least now I know it *was* a good plan.

I slowly start to walk away, and the rest follow my lead. Felicia catches up to me. "How were you ever going to pay for it, Graham?" she asks tentatively, and I get that she's trying to tread carefully on a very delicate situation.

I guess it doesn't matter if I tell her now. "Casey was going to lend me the money." I shrug. "I was going to get a job and pay him back."

Felicia smiles. "That's sweet," she says, and then pauses before she finishes her sentence, "but, you know, Roxana wouldn't have wanted you to do that. . . ."

"Yeah, that's true," Samira, who is now flanking me on the other side, agrees. "She's too practical sometimes."

I blink rapidly. So what are the girls trying to tell me? That I was doomed to fail no matter what?

It's too raw and fresh to feel okay about that now, but maybe that's a kindness on their part. Maybe it'll help me stop blaming myself . . . someday.

As we head toward the Batmobile parked in the distance, my heart stutters at the sight of the short-haired girl and her tall British companion waiting there for us. I think that day may be very far away.

Chapter 22
METAL DETECTION

WE SPEND SOME TIME AT THE DC DISPLAY, LOOKING AT THE MOVIE PROPS.
When I get to Michael Keaton's Batman costume, I feel compelled to text Amelia a picture.

Look. It's your man's threads, I write.

Swoon! she writes back a few moments later.

One of DC's star writers is doing a signing, and a huge line winds around and around the glass cases, so it's a little hard to get close to some of the other displays. I nearly mow down a guy with a faux-hawk and glasses standing beside one of the cases, looking a bit forlornly at the writer greeting his fans. I'm guessing he wasn't able to get a ticket himself. Yesterday, I would have known exactly how he feels. Today, I am so beyond that.

Afterward, the six of us wander the show floor for a while, one or another of us browsing various kiosks and booths. Samira buys an *Adventure Time* T-shirt, and it's while we're waiting to pay that I notice a small brunette girl enthusiastically waving at me from the booth across the aisle. I squint, and it takes me a moment to recognize her. It's Louisa, my lovelorn counterpart from speed dating, the one who was sort of stalking her ex-boyfriend. I smile and wave back.

She's holding hands with a short, slightly chubby guy who is clutching a sheet of paper and raising his hand in the air while he stares intently at the guy behind the booth. His back is to me, so I feel comfortable mouthing my question to Louisa. *Your ex?*

A slow blush creeps across her face and she sends me an almost guilty grin in return as she shakes her head. *Speed dating,* she mouths back, adding a helpless shrug.

I laugh and then look at the two of them again. After a moment, there's a round of applause and I hear the guy behind the booth point to Louisa's new dude and say, "You are the winner of this round of trivia. Pick your prize!"

He turns to Louisa and smiles triumphantly. "You pick." She beams at him and I watch as she selects a small, plush Ninja Turtle. Then she hugs him, her laughing eyes meeting mine over his shoulder.

She certainly doesn't look like the tortured person I met two days ago . . . but I bet I do. I bet I look exactly the same.

I smile at her anyway and give her a thumbs-up and a friendly wave by way of good-bye. She does the same, and then I turn back around, trudging after my friends and the albatross I haven't been as lucky as Louisa to shake off.

About ten minutes later, as Samira is debating whether to go to a *Star Wars* origami panel that starts soon, Devin turns to Roxana and me. "Hey, don't you guys have your critique session soon? From that Breaking into Comics panel?"

"Oh, right," Roxana says vaguely. "That."

I stare at her. So that's it, then. All our years of working on *Misfits* together has been boiled down to "that"? How could I not see how right Roxana was about everything changing? How could I have been so stupid as to believe this could ever work between us?

"I can take Samira to the origami panel," Felicia volunteers.

"Me too," Casey says, and I can't help but stare at him incredulously, knowing full well the origami panel is not filling up a cell in his spreadsheet.

"Sam, is that okay?" Roxana asks.

"Sure." Samira nods. "The panel ends at one fifteen. When will you guys be done?"

"Um . . . I think our slot was at twelve forty-five," Roxana says. "And it's only fifteen minutes."

"Okay, so meet you a little after one fifteen?" Felicia asks. "Maybe at the food court?"

They all agree and finalize our plans, and no one seems to notice that this whole time, I haven't said a word. They can decide my immediate future. Hell, if they want, they can decide my distant future, too. Nothing is in my control anyway, why bother pretending it is? Why not leave everything up to everyone else's whims?

The group breaks up, and I straggle behind Devin and Roxana as they head toward the critique room. But when we get near the escalators, Devin stops. "I'm actually going to go check out the Adam Hughes signing. Meet you at one fifteen also?"

"Oh," Roxana says, clearly taken aback. "Sure."

Devin smiles and quickly squeezes her shoulder. "See you soon," he says as he hops on the escalator.

We watch his tall form drift away from us, I think both hit with the uncomfortable realization that we're finally alone together again. Well, alone in a sea of thousands. Which, surprisingly, is still really awkward.

We do a sort of weird dance as we walk toward the panel room, neither one of us quite wanting to walk next to the other, but feeling like it's too weird to walk too far apart, either.

Finally, as we're only a few steps from the room, Roxana breaks the silence. "So, are you nervous?"

About what? Us? Last night? I look down at her blankly.

"You know, getting workshopped by Donnelly and Park." She reads my confused expression correctly and clarifies.

Oh, right. That. "Sure," I say even though, truthfully, I haven't given it a single thought since the moment we dropped our pages off yesterday.

"I wonder what they'll think," she says as we enter the room.

"Yeah. Me too."

And then, allowing myself to concentrate for just a moment on what's about to happen, I realize that I *am* nervous about it. We worked really hard on those panels and that issue in particular, revising and rewriting it a few times. I know objectively that it's some of Roxana's best work. But it's almost impossible to ever be that objective about my own work. I wonder if it really and truly is any good.

An NYCC staffer comes over and makes sure our names are on her clipboard. She tells us to take a seat and we'll get called up. "They're pretty much running on schedule, so they should be seeing you between twelve forty-five and twelve fifty," she tells us.

We sit down in one of the rows of chairs that are still set up panel-style and watch from far away as Morgan Donnelly and Brandon Park animatedly speak to a guy with a ponytail about his work. I tap my foot nervously; Roxana touches her hair. Things are otherwise quiet between us.

"Graham?"

I turn around and see Amelia standing there beside another girl with short, spiky pigtails. Amelia is wearing a green jumpsuit and has dyed her left ear green. In other words, she's dressed as Althena as Ripley from *Alien*. I grin at her.

"Hey! Nice costume!" I say.

She smiles back. "This is Joanna." She introduces her friend to Roxana and me and we murmur greetings. It's only then that I notice Amelia is clutching a few sheets of paper.

"What are you doing here?" I ask. "Did you get critiqued?"

Amelia nods. "Yeah, something small." She moves the typed pages away from her chest, and I can see some scrawls on it in red pen.

"I didn't see you at their panel yesterday," I say.

"I was at the one on Friday," she replies.

"Ah." I nod toward her pages. "How was it?"

She breaks out into a grin. "Nerve-wracking. But fun. They took it really seriously, and that's nice, you know. Like they were giving me actual, thoughtful critiques, not treating me like I was some fragile, dumb kid."

"That's great!" I say, even though it's also ratcheted up my nerves.

"Did you want to go to the NYU information session? It's starting soon," Joanna says to Amelia.

"Oh, yes," she responds, and then turns to me again. "Maybe I'll text you later and we can all meet up?"

"Sure." I smile back at her. She and Joanna say their good-byes and turn to leave.

A few moments later, a voice next to me finally pipes up.

"You seem chummy. You just met yesterday, right?"

What the hell? Like Roxana is one to talk.

"Um, Friday," I say, and can't help adding, "just like you and Devin, actually." Exactly like that, in fact.

She looks stung, and she opens and closes her mouth a few times. "I didn't mean . . . ," she starts, but then our names are called and we find ourselves sitting side by side in front of Morgan and Brandon. I guess our body language isn't too inviting, because Morgan makes a comment.

"Don't look so defensive, guys," he says casually. "You won't need armor for this, I promise."

He smiles and takes out our pages, double-checking that *The Misfits of Mage High* is ours. We nod, and then the two of them start talking, both of them extolling the virtues of our work first. Morgan tells me my writing is crisp and funny and I have a good sense of comedic timing and characterization. Brandon says Roxana's art is fresh and bold and that the best part is that both the art and the writing seem to be doing equal amounts of work in moving the story along, essential in the comic world. "You guys are clearly a really great team," Brandon says.

I try to take that for the compliment it is, instead of feeling the sting that comes with wondering if that sentence should really be in the past tense.

Then the two gently but firmly give us some suggestions on what we could improve. Morgan thinks I might want to concentrate a little more on accelerating the plot, maybe pare down some of the jokes that might be taking up too much valuable real estate in terms of telling the story. Brandon talks a little bit about Roxana's use of color and how she might want to think about where she wants the viewer's eye to be drawn in each panel. He singles out how one particular panel lacks some focus, and gives her some advice on how she might be able to fix that.

As Brandon is finishing up illustrating his point to Roxana, Morgan's phone buzzes and his screen lights up. "Whoops, sorry about that!" he says, and immediately hits a key to shut it down. But not before I catch a glimpse of his wallpaper.

It's an enormous horned demon standing in a room full of treasure, looking furious and imposing. I recognize it instantly because I've spent the past five years searching eagerly for it on the Z-men forums. It's the same image as copper670's avatar, the user I was convinced was Zinc in disguise.

I gape at the blank screen where the image appeared, and when Morgan asks if we have any questions, I just know I have to speak up. "Yes. This is a weird one, but . . ." I stare up at him. "Are you copper670? On the Z-men message boards?"

Shock crosses his face, followed by a surprised grin, neither of which he can hide fast enough. Which I guess he realizes, because after a moment he says, "Oh, man . . . you found me out."

"Oh my God!" Roxy squeals, and we stare at each other, aware that we've just solved an enduring mystery.

"We just really love your fan fic on there," I immediately gush. "It's our favorite."

Roxana nods. "In fact, Graham has been swearing up and down that copper670 is really Zinc. Incognito."

Morgan laughs. "I wish!"

"It's just that good. Seriously!" I defend my assumption. "Though, of course, you are a professional writer. So that makes sense." I look over a bit smugly at Roxy. Like I was a little right.

She laughs and gives me a small nod of acknowledgment.

"I hate to break up the sleuthing party, much as I'm enjoying this," Brandon says, "but I'm afraid our time is up."

"Oh," I say as I stand. "Thank you so much. You guys were so helpful."

"Yes," Roxana says. "We really appreciate it." We shake their hands, and Roxana grabs our panels as we leave the table.

Heading out of the room, she turns to me. "How did you—"

"I saw the wallpaper on his phone!" I burst out. "It was his avatar."

She laughs. "Nice work, Sherlock." The highest of compliments.

"Thank you, John." I give a little bow.

"So I guess we're not killing off Slammerghini," she teases. Oh, right. The bet.

"Right," I say slowly. "I guess you win. But I forgot what you asked for, actually."

"I'm not sure I had decided yet. . . ." Roxy's voice trails off, and she's staring into the distance. I wonder if she's remembering it too, the moment I almost kissed her. Maybe now, after everything that's happened, she's seeing it in a different light.

Devin is waiting for us right outside the room. "How did the critique go?" He pounces as soon as he sees us.

I leave Roxana to answer him however she sees fit.

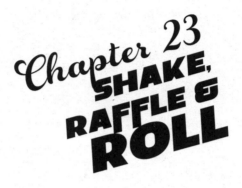

Chapter 23
SHAKE, RAFFLE & ROLL

WE EACH END UP AT DIFFERENT LINES AT THE FOOD COURT—I'M FEELING LIKE a gyro today—but manage to snag two tables near each other. Felicia, Casey, and I sit at one and Roxana, Devin, and Samira at the other.

There isn't too much time before Samira's fan fiction panel, which Roxana says she wants to take her to, so the other group is wolfing down their food. I'm wondering if I should go with them, especially once Devin reveals he has other plans for the afternoon.

"You don't remember what's happening at two thirty?" Casey asks me when I mention this.

"No idea," I say.

He stares at me, incredulous. "Um, the toy reveal? For *Star Wars*?"

Oh, right. This is a big deal because they're going to reveal one of the brand-new characters in the latest movie via its action figure. Which, of course, I am hereditarily obligated to be very interested in.

After making sure that Samira doesn't particularly care whether I accompany them to her panel or not, I agree to check out the toy reveal. Felicia opts to go with us but asks if we can make a quick detour to the bathroom.

While Casey and I wait for her outside, I see my opportunity and ask about the two of them hanging out so much today.

"I've been trying to find out her weak point all day!" he says, clearly frustrated. "I thought there had to be something I could exploit for my own GPA gain. But there's nothing. She really is damn perfect."

I laugh. "Oh, is that what you've been doing all day?" I ask, and then, in a burst of inspiration, add, "You know she told me on Friday how funny she thinks you are?"

"Funny?" he says, blinking. "Oh, like, weird."

"No, dude. Funny. As in humorous and amusing."

His eyebrows crinkle in confusion. "Really?"

"Really. I think you've managed to charm her." I refrain from adding the *somehow*, but then the skeptical look on his face prompts me to ask, "What's the matter, Case? You were all gung ho about Callie, and I think we both know that would have gone down in flames before it even started. Felicia is amazing, actually knows you exist . . . and seems to like you."

Casey frowns and fidgets. "I don't think that can possibly be true," he mutters.

He looks so uncomfortable that it finally hits me. Of course, Callie is totally unattainable and he knows that—in fact, that's probably her appeal. Someone he can safely worship from afar. The thought of Felicia in front of him is terrifying. A real girl who might like him back? A real opportunity for romance? That's something he can't at all control.

A very small part of me wonders if I haven't been doing the same thing with Roxy. If I haven't always known she wouldn't return my romantic feelings. Did I make her the subject of my fantasies on purpose? But then again, so much about it seemed right and perfect. Like we fit so well as friends that it shouldn't have been this difficult to take it to the next level, just like Samira mentioned. I feel like this really was a story with an ending I could not have predicted—still can't predict.

Felicia comes out of the bathroom. "Ready?" she asks us, throwing a smile in Casey's direction. He nods and then starts to briskly walk away, only Felicia keeps up with him. I watch her lean in to ask him to explain the significance of the toy reveal to her, and I have to smile as I hear his rushed response.

So maybe some nerd really *will* find love at Comic Con . . . it just won't happen to be me.

My phone buzzes and I take it out to read a text from Amelia. **Did you hear about the Zinc make-good?!**

I text her back a question mark and she sends me a link.

A dedicated page on the New York Comic Con website explains that to apologize for the mishap at the line for Friday's Zinc event, the NYCC organizers and the film studio are offering a make-good. There will be a special screening of the first twenty minutes of the upcoming *The Chronicles of Althena* movie, followed by a Q&A with director Solomon Pierce-Johnson. Tickets will be given away via a raffle starting at two o'clock. Everyone who shows up in person at the studio's booth will get one raffle ticket. Unless you have a log-in to z-men.net with a history of having posted on there for the past three months. Then they will give you two raffle tickets.

Holy shit.

"Halt!" I yell out to Casey and Felicia immediately, and then explain to them what I've just read. "I think this calls for an emergency schedule switch," I say to Casey, whose expression looks like he's really grappling with the idea.

But after a moment, he seems to pull himself together. "Yes, I think you're right," he says. We change course to head over to the studio's booth. On the way, I text Roxy to tell her what's happened, though I don't think she'll be getting out of Samira's panel until three.

When we get there, there's a line snaking around the booth, but it seems to be moving pretty fast, and I notice that an extraordinary number of both studio employees and NYCC staffers are manning this thing. Clearly, they're not taking any chances this time.

The registration process involves using the booth's iPads to log into a

Z-men account, if you have one, and they really do seem to be checking to make sure you're an active member and not someone who just signed up ten minutes ago. Then they scan ID badges to make sure there aren't people trying to scam the system by getting on line multiple times, and they give you one or two raffle tickets, depending on your qualifications. "Be in Room 1C04 at three p.m.," the girl who gives me the tickets says. "If your number is called, you have to be there in person to get a ticket for the screening."

I hold on as tight to my two tickets as Charlie Bucket, and then wait while Casey gets two and Felicia gets one. If I knew Roxy's Z-men password, I would have had Felicia log in as her, but, alas, I do not.

"If I win, I'll give mine to Roxana," Felicia tells me as soon as she gets off the line.

"Thanks," I tell her.

She looks like she's about to say something but then just shakes her head and smiles instead. "Proxy you're welcome," she finally responds.

Casey glances at his watch. "I think there might be time to see at least a little bit of the toy reveal," he says.

But I'm not taking any chances this time. "You go ahead," I tell him. "I think I want to head over to the raffle room. Just to be safe."

"I think I'll go with Graham," Felicia responds, and I'm genuinely surprised she's not going to leave with Casey. But then again, maybe I shouldn't be. Maybe I should give up trying to figure anything out in the romance department, for myself or anyone else. Perhaps there's something to be said for just sticking with what I know.

As the two of us start to walk toward Room 1C04, I'm suddenly struck by an unpleasant thought. But it's important enough to voice it.

"Hey, Felicia. Can you do me a favor?"

"Hmmm?"

"Can you text Roxy the info about the raffle? Just in case she's blocked my number or something and doesn't get my text?" I vaguely look in the direction of my phone.

"Graham," Felicia says gently, "she didn't block your number."

"I know it's not likely," I concede, "but I just want to make sure she gets this message. You know, things are so weird between us."

She takes out her phone then and sends a message. "It's just for your peace of mind. But honestly, I know she wouldn't do that." She hesitates for a moment, choosing her words. "Everything will be okay. I think she's just in shock."

"Yeah," I say. This was exactly what Samira said. "I just wish it wasn't so shocking to have someone like me love her."

"But, Graham, this isn't about someone *like* you. This is about *you*. Like, you, her very best friend," Felicia protests. "You guys have been a particular unit for a long time, and that's something that's really special to her. And yes, I admit, you've probably been put in a compartment. But it's an important compartment. And now you want to go somewhere else and . . . well, that's hard."

I think about what she's saying, as objectively as I possibly can. And I can see her point. If Roxana really had no idea how I felt and I blindsided her—then maybe shock wouldn't be too far a leap as a reaction.

"So do you really think we can be friends again? Like before?"

Felicia mulls this over. "Well, yes. And no. I think your friendship will survive. But I don't know if everything is going to be *exactly* like it was before. But come on, Graham—when is that ever true? We're all constantly changing and evolving and growing up. You're a writer. You should get that more than anyone."

I nod, letting the wisdom of her words sink in and settle. It's not like they're a cure-all salve, because it's not like I can just shut off my feelings for Roxy. But it's something to chew on anyway.

"Damn, Felicia," I finally say to her with a small laugh. "You have everything figured out. You really are perfect."

I expect her to shrug or smile or say something else profound, but she immediately frowns. "Who told you that?" she asks.

I laugh again. "Casey. Me. Um, everyone, actually."

But Felicia isn't laughing. "Casey, too?" She lets out a puff of air. "I'm *not* perfect," she says sharply.

Oh, crap, I've clearly said the wrong thing. "I'm sorry . . . ," I start.

But Felicia sighs. "It's just . . . I've heard that before, and I know it's meant to be a compliment or something, but actually it's a huge burden. It's like setting me up to fail."

"Felicia, have you ever failed at anything in your life?"

"Of course I have!" she replies. "Maybe not like tests, but I've had friends who've dumped me, and sports I've been terrible at, and crushes who didn't like me back. . . ."

"You have?" I ask, and I'm truly surprised. Which crush would not like Felicia back?

Felicia shakes her head and rolls her eyes. "No one can live up to perfect, Graham. Not me. Not Roxana. Seriously, you guys need to stop this nonsense. Maybe if you let yourself see us as we really are—you know, human—you wouldn't let yourself get so intimidated. You wouldn't be setting *yourself* up to fail."

Yikes! I decide not to mention to her that Felicia Obayashi giving me a lecture is, by its very nature, intimidating. But she might also have a point.

We've reached the raffle room, which must be one of the Javits's biggest conference rooms. There are no chairs set up here, just a stage with a podium, and the empty space makes the room look particularly massive. There are already a couple hundred people congregating, and I immediately recognize one very unwelcome Papa Smurf hat among them. "Let's be honest. Friday's panel didn't inspire much confidence in this movie, did it?" the owner of the hat is droning loudly to his friend.

You have got to be kidding me.

But just as I feel my eyes burning with the desire to create a thundercloud right above that horrendous hat, a cheerful voice calls out, "You made it!" and I turn to see Amelia and Joanna approaching us.

"Yes!" I say, waving my raffle tickets and feeling happy for the distraction from the social injustice of *that guy* being here. "Just in time. Thanks a billion for the text."

"Of course!" she says, and smiles at me. "I hope you get in."

I realize Amelia and Felicia weren't properly introduced before, so I do the honors.

"Are you a big Zinc fan too?" Amelia asks.

"Not really," Felicia says. "But if I win, I think I know of a few I can sell my ticket to for an exorbitant price." She winks to show she's kidding, and Amelia laughs.

"You could definitely make some quick cash," Amelia says.

"You're right, you're not perfect. You're evil," I say to Felicia.

"*Mwahahahaha,*" she responds, her villainous laugh way more impressive than I would ever have expected.

"The casting is a total joke." Papa Smurf's obnoxious voice rings through the room again. "Please. I mean, Malcolm Vreeland? Really? Everyone knows musicians can't act. Plus how are they going to get around all the plot holes the original series already has?"

"Is that guy for real?" Amelia asks incredulously. I look at her appalled face and immediately feel relieved that someone can share in my disgust.

"You have no idea," I tell her before I go on to explain his behavior on the Zinc line, how he was part of the bum rush, and how he got into the Zinc panel anyway.

"There should be a special place in nerd hell for guys like that," Amelia declares once I'm done with my story.

"Agreed. Like he has to spend all of infinity stuck in his most hated fandom."

"Complete with plot holes," Amelia adds, eyes gleaming.

"And miscast actors."

"Only he's now a mute—and can't say a damned thing about it."

"And also armless, so he couldn't go type anything on a forum, either."

"Only there are no forums . . . except for the gushy kind. And *only* the gushy kind," she finishes with a flourish. "Emoji hearts everywhere."

I grin.

In a few minutes, we're joined by Casey, who, somehow, also has Devin in tow. It's almost three and still no sign of Roxana. She must be sticking the fan fiction panel out to the end. I hope she at least got one of our messages.

"How was the toy reveal?" I ask Casey.

He sighs. "They blabbed on and on so long I had to leave before they actually showed off the figure," he says, clearly frustrated.

I indicate Devin with my head and lower my voice. "How did you pick him up again?"

Casey shrugs. "He was headed this way. I bumped into him near the room. Said he heard about the raffle just in time and snagged a ticket."

Of course he did. I wish you had to answer a trivia question or something before getting a raffle ticket. At least that way they could separate out the true fans who should actually be the ones getting into this make-good.

"Okay, everyone," an older man wearing a movie merch *Althena* T-shirt says from the mic at the front of the room. "Let's get this part done as quickly and efficiently as possible. The screening will start at three fifteen and we will escort the raffle winners straight from here."

He presses a button on the laptop he has up on his podium. A series of about a hundred numbers comes up on the screen behind him. "These are the winning raffle numbers, picked at random by the computer," he continues. "They're in numeric order, so take a look at your tickets. If you have a winning number, please form a line here, to my right, and one of our staffers will take care of you." He indicates the five people, also in official *Althena* movie merchandise, who are standing just below the stage.

From all around me, I start to hear groans and sighs of disappointment, and I'm delighted to see that Papa Smurf's is one of them. Satisfied that there is some justice in the world, I join everyone else in examining our tickets, squinting up at the board, trying to find a match.

Neither Amelia, Joanna, Felicia, Casey, nor Devin has a winning ticket.

But I do.

0389213.

I stare at the number in my hand and then at the number on the screen, back and forth, just to make sure I haven't developed some sort of late-onset dyslexia. It's Felicia who notices first, how the rest of them have all claimed they didn't win, but I have just turned into a statue who can't stop staring at the piece of paper in my hand.

"Did you win?" she asks me.

I look up at her and slowly nod.

"Oh my God!" she squeals. "Graham won!" she tells the rest of the group, and Amelia and Joanna both shout in delight. Casey calls out, "Awesome!" and even Devin slaps me on the back.

"Yes!" Amelia says. "I'm so glad it was you. You deserved it after Friday."

I smile at her slowly, but I'm still numb to my extraordinary good luck. And then a familiar voice comes from behind us.

"I got your message," Roxana calls out breathlessly. "What happened? Anyone win?" She and Samira both look like they sprinted over here.

"Graham did," Casey says.

Our eyes meet. Roxana's face breaks out into a genuine smile. "Oh my God! That's great."

"You should go get in line, man," Devin says, pointing toward the stage.

But I feel rooted to my spot, and I can't stop staring at Roxy. Despite everything going to hell, this weekend was supposed to be all about making her happy.

The raffle ticket is still perched on my hand, and I look down at it, suddenly aware of a stunning truth. As much as Zinc means to me; as much as I nerd out over every bit of his oeuvre, or every new bit of gossip or paraphernalia that pops up online; as much as I'm obsessed by every aspect of it . . . I don't even want to have this experience without Roxana.

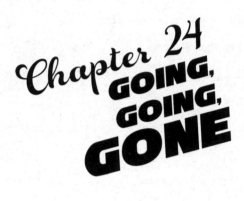

Chapter 24
GOING, GOING, GONE

"HERE. YOU TAKE THIS." I GRAB ROXY'S HAND AND SLAP THE WINNING RAFFLE ticket into it before she realizes what's happening.

She stares down at it and then back up at me. "What are you doing? I can't take this."

"You have to," I say firmly.

She sputters out a laugh. "I have to?"

I nod. I've made up my mind, and there's nothing she can say to change it. "I want you to."

She stares at me, the ticket still lying on her open, outstretched hand. "But why? Zinc is your all-time favorite writer, Graham."

"And he's your all-time favorite artist," I respond calmly.

She shakes her head. "You won the ticket fair and square." She goes to put the ticket back in my hand, but I hold my hands behind me, out of her reach.

"I don't care."

"Stop being ridiculous!" she says as she struggles to grab my arm. But being about nine inches taller than her is coming in handy at the moment.

"Look," I say, my arms held up in the air as if in surrender. "If you don't take it, I'm just going to give it away to someone else here. Someone random. I'm serious."

She finally stops trying to grab my hands. "I don't understand. Why are you doing this?"

I realize that Felicia, Casey, Samira, Devin, Amelia, and even Joanna are staring at us, but I have to tell her the truth anyway. Without alcohol this time and with an audience. "I wanted you to have the perfect weekend," I confess. "Everything's gone wrong. But this is the one thing that hasn't. So please. Take it. For me."

Roxana's big brown eyes stare into mine, and I wonder if she can tell I'm near tears. Whatever she sees there makes her look down at the raffle ticket one more time before asking me, "Are you sure?"

"Positive."

"Okay," she finally says as she closes her hand around the ticket, and I let out a breath I didn't know I was holding. "But I just . . . I don't know how to thank you . . ."

"Just get on that line. Quickly," I say as I point to the line of winners in the front, which has already started moving.

"Oh," she says hurriedly, and turns to head toward it. After a moment, she turns back and calls to me, "I'll try to remember everything, so I can tell you all about it."

"You better. Everything."

She nods, and for a moment, I picture us in her backyard, her giving me every minute detail of the screening. And it's almost normal between us. For now, I'll have to take it, that hope that it will be.

Before she turns back to her line, she glimpses her sister. "Sam? Are you going to be okay with the rest of the group for an hour?"

"Of course!" Samira yells back. "See you after."

Roxana still looks dazed as she glances over at us one last time and then, finally, gets on the back of the line. Only a few moments later, a staffer comes over and scans her raffle ticket before handing her a different pass. Then Roxy shuffles with the rest of the line through a door at the back of the room.

I imagine the rest of the group is still staring at me, but I'm luckily saved from any further inquiries by blessed Felicia's cheerful voice. "So, what's next on the agenda?" she asks.

Casey pulls out his spreadsheet and takes a look. "Actually, I have a forty-five-minute lull," he says. He takes out his regular Comic Con schedule and hands it to Felicia. "Anything here look interesting to you?"

Way to go, Case, I think, impressed by his gesture . . . even if Felicia doesn't quite yet grasp the significance of his giving her control over the schedule like that. She casually looks at her watch and then starts to read some options out loud. "Three thirty. We have a WWE Wrestlers Panel. LGBT in Comics panel. Designing a Board Game. The Sun Auction starts . . ."

"Oh!" I say. "How about we check that out?" Both Felicia and Samira peer at me intently. "I swear I won't buy anything," I say with a smile. "But an auction might be fun to watch."

"I'm game," Casey says.

"Okay, let's do it, then," Felicia says.

I ask Amelia and Joanna if they want to come along, and they accept. Almost as an afterthought, I realize it would be terribly rude not to also ask Devin, who says he'll tag along.

There's too many of us to walk together through the crowd, so we end up sort of paired up and staggered. Felicia and Casey walk ahead of Samira and me. Somewhere behind me, I hear Devin start up a conversation with Amelia and Joanna. Naturally.

"Hey, that was really sweet. What you did with the ticket," Samira says to me quietly. "If I was writing this in a story, she definitely would've kissed you after that."

I smile down at her. "Then I wish I was in one of your stories." And who wouldn't wish that? Certainly everyone here—dressed up as aliens, and wizards, and zombies, and superheroes—wants desperately to be inside a story, to be part of something more logical and meaningful than real life seems to be. Because even worlds with dragons and time machines seem to be more ordered than our own. When you live for stories, when you spend so much of your time immersed in careful constructs of three and five acts, it sometimes feels like you're just stumbling through the rest of life, trying to divine meaningful narrative threads from the chaos. Which, as I learned the hard way this weekend, can be painfully fruitless. Fiction is there when real life fails you. But it's not a substitute.

We finally get to the auction spot, another large room that's down a very long hallway from the raffle room. The front is mostly filled, but there are still some empty rows near the back, and we file into one of those. I end up with Samira on one side and Amelia on the other.

There are a lot of different things being auctioned, everything from old artwork, to exclusive sketches done on the show floor, to props and memorabilia. A chair from the set of *Star Trek: Voyager* goes for almost ten grand. Conversely, a small but beautiful sketch of Harley Quinn by Jim Lee is practically a steal at $150.

At one point, Amelia hits me in the arm and excitedly points out the lot that's coming up next: the small collection of original Zinc work.

I nod at her, and I know we're both seething with envy as we see the two covers get some aggressive bids and counterbids, with the more iconic cover finally going for almost eight thousand dollars and the other one for nearly four thousand.

"Do you think if I paid that guy twenty bucks, he'd let me just hold the cover for five seconds?" Amelia whispers to me.

"You'll never know if you don't ask," I whisper back.

"Good point."

And then the final piece of the Zinc collection comes up and I watch as five people go head-to-head on what just yesterday I was sure I could make mine. The page gets a starting bid of $750 immediately, and within thirty seconds, it's up to $3,000. A few people eventually drop out of the race, and our heads all bounce back and forth as we see an older, rotund lady and a skinny hipster with a Fu Manchu mustache duke it out all the way to the bitter end.

It goes on for a good while, the room practically silent from held breaths, but finally, the hipster relents, and the lady snags the piece for $7,750.

There is thunderous applause, and both contenders look flushed and sweaty, but the winner has a huge smile plastered on her face.

Casey leans across Samira to speak to me. "It's all for the best. It would've taken you forever to pay me off!"

That's true, but is it really all for the best?

Maybe. And maybe one day I'll be able to see that too.

"'Sometimes all we have is the knowledge that something extraordinary exists in the universe, even if we can't be the ones to claim it. Sometimes that has to be enough,'" Amelia says, quoting Althena. My jaw drops and I wonder if all my thoughts are that transparent. It takes her looking wistfully at the auction winner to make me realize that she's talking about the *Althena* pages. But she could just as easily have been talking about Roxana and me.

Somehow I've found yet another connection to Robert Zinc's words. Despite everything, I have to marvel at that. After all, it's not every day that one finds yet another dungeon to explore deep in the heart of his most beloved fandom.

Chapter 25
A NEW HOPE

THE AUCTION IS STILL GOING ON AT A LITTLE BEFORE FOUR, AND CASEY LETS US
know there's a screening and panel he wants to get to that starts at
four. "It's for a new pilot, a show called *Mr. Advantageous*."

"Oh!" Samira chimes in. "That's the one with Tim Fisher, right? Will
he be there?"

Casey glances at his schedule. "Yup."

"I'm in for that," Samira says, eyes flashing in the giddy way of
eleven-year-old girls.

"Me too," Felicia says, and I notice her expression isn't too different.

"Okay," Casey says as he turns to me. "You?"

Actually, I was just about to suggest getting out of here anyway, but not for *Mr. Advantageous*. "I think Roxana should be getting out of the screening soon. I might go hang around that room so she can give me the scoop."

"Oh, that sounds good! Mind if I go with you?" Amelia asks.

"Not at all," I say.

"I'll come too," Devin chimes in, and I take note that he didn't even ask.

Joanna says she has to head home to study for a precalc test, so she splits for the exit, while Casey, Felicia, and Samira part ways with us a little bit farther along the hallway.

Amelia and I are walking in step, but I'm aware of Devin's tall shadow looming behind us.

"So, Graham," Amelia says. "I've been meaning to ask you something."

"What's that?"

"I'm going to be blunt, because, well, I'm a city chick. But is there something going on between you and Roxana?"

I start. I was not expecting that. I stare down at Amelia, who's waiting patiently for my answer, and I laugh nervously before I give it to her. "Nope. Nothing," I finally say. Because there isn't.

Amelia pauses. "But do you want there to be?" she asks shrewdly.

I'm speechless for a minute. I also realize that behind us, Devin, who up to this point has been messing around on his phone, is now keenly listening.

"I did," I finally admit.

"Did?" Amelia asks.

"Do," I correct myself after taking a moment to think it over. "But it's not going to happen, I don't think. So I'm trying to get over it." I smile down at her with a faint shrug.

She looks at me piercingly before she speaks again. "Well, I appreciate the honesty."

"Ah, honesty. It's my fatal flaw."

"Truthfully, I appreciate a lot of things about you, Graham," Amelia continues.

"You do?"

"Of course," she says as she stays in step beside me but keeps looking up at me. "You're smart and funny and crazy talented. And we have a lot in common. Not to mention, I think you're hot."

I stop short, my mouth gaping. Devin bumps into me from behind, but I don't care. "You think I'm . . . wait. What?"

I honestly had no idea where this conversation was going, but I can truthfully say I was not expecting this. I stare at this girl—no, scratch that—this *beautiful* girl who just told me she thinks I'm hot, and for the next ten seconds, I'm pretty sure I'm about to wake up from this admittedly fantastic dream.

"Please," Amelia says with a smirk. "Piercing blue eyes. Thick black glasses. You've got a total Clark Kent/Superman vibe going on." She grins at me, and I involuntarily touch my glasses, amazed that they actually seem to have served their intended purpose. "Are you really telling me you don't know when a girl likes you?"

I let out a short burst of laughter. She can't possibly fathom how accurate she is with that observation. "I can say with one hundred percent certainty that—much like Jon Snow—I know nothing when it comes to that department." I smile shyly down at her.

"Well, to make it clear . . . I like you, Graham."

We've stopped walking, and we're sort of in the middle of the hallway, but I'm too floored to contemplate etiquette right now. People stream around us like we're a boulder stuck in their stream, and if they curse at us or even elbow us, I truly don't notice.

Forget beautiful. Amelia is brave, too. It only took three months, a lot of alcohol, and an annoying British guy for me to work up the nerve to tell the person I know best in the world that I love her. And this girl is laying it all out there for a near stranger.

"So I guess I want to know if you want to go out with me sometime," she finishes.

I stare at her, this girl who is *not* Roxy. I hardly know her at all. I don't know her favorite foods or her least-favorite subject. I don't know her comfort movie or even if she has one. I have no idea how many freckles are on her nose. And she knows just as little about me; I'm not her best friend. But then again, I'm not like a brother to her, either. As Felicia put it, I haven't been put in that compartment.

And now she's waiting for an answer. "I . . . yes. Sometime," I say without overthinking it. I'm surprised by my own words, but I also immediately know they're the right ones. Yes, sometime, someday, and probably soon, I'll be ready to get to know Amelia. I think I'll want to try to start something together, on the same page, knowing we're reaching for something more than friendship right from the start. What a novel concept.

She smiles up at me, and we're close enough that I can count the freckles on her nose. There are seven.

"That sounds like an honest answer. See, one of your strong points." She lightly reaches out and touches my hand, and I'm surprised by how exotic that feels—warm and slightly electric. Instinctively, I take my thumb and sweep it gently once over the back of her hand. And that feels pretty great too.

We grin at each other, not noticing that the door to one of the rooms a bit down the hallway has opened up and people are streaming out. I don't even see the short-haired brunette girl who's made a beeline for us until she's right at my elbow.

"Oh my gosh, you guys." Roxana is breathless. "Althena. The way she looked. Fiona Ruthers is *exactly* the right person to play her. And Noth. I know we were all skeptical about Malcolm Vreeland, but he totally surprised me. It was perfect . . ." She stops midsentence and I can tell she's assessing something. Even though Amelia and I have sprung apart and aren't touching anymore, maybe it's how close we're still standing to each other.

I finally feel conscious enough of my surroundings to pull us all over to the side of the hallway.

"Tell me more, tell me more," Devin sings at Roxana, and she looks at him, blinking. Almost like she forgot about him. Then she looks back up at me, her eyes questioning.

I put on a smile. "Right. You said you'd tell me everything." I say it mildly, but an accusation hangs in the air nonetheless: You said you'd tell *me* . . .

I think of what I imagined, us sitting in her backyard just like on the countless days we've done that before, and I realize that just like every other perfect scene I've fantasized about, it's gone. It's never going to happen; it never was. "Tell *us* everything," I amend, trying to put a bandage on it.

Roxy looks at me, and for a moment, I think she sees it too—the image of the two of us in her backyard, vanishing in a puff of smoke.

But she does start to talk. "Well, the rock star thing actually worked for Malcolm as Noth," she says, referencing the musician's acting debut. "Just because Noth is supposed to be so mysterious and aloof. And after a couple of minutes, I stopped flinching every time he opened his mouth to say a line. He's actually totally believable. And the costumes and sets were really great. Almost exactly how I pictured them."

"How was the Solomon Pierce-Johnson Q&A?" Amelia asks. "He helped inspire confidence in the movie, right?"

Roxana seems to study Amelia before answering. "Yes, actually.

That's a good way of putting it," she agrees slowly. "He is definitely an Althena fanboy, and he knows his stuff, so it felt like the thing is in good hands. Oh! They did change around some timeline stuff. That scene with Althena and the ice cream cone comes within the first ten minutes." She looks at me expectantly.

I think about it. "Hmmm. That's kinda hard to process when you know the story so well, but . . . I can kinda see how that might work? To establish the Ezula mode of communication earlier?"

"Yeah, exactly," Roxana agrees. "It was kind of jarring, but when I thought about it after, I could see why they would do it that way. Anyway, I wish I could see the rest of the movie *right now*. I'm much more excited for it now than I was before."

"That is definitely promising, coming from you," Amelia says.

"Definitely," I agree, and though a part of me listens to the rest of the conversation about the movie, a part is also highly aware of the very strange situation I'm currently in: here is the girl whom I professed my unrequited love to yesterday, and here is another girl who just professed her crush on me. It's definitely enough to make a geek's mind explode.

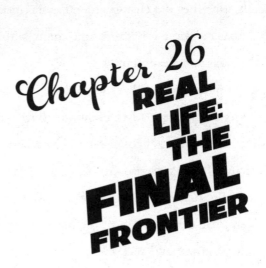

Chapter 26
REAL LIFE: THE FINAL FRONTIER

"I HATE TO SAY THIS, BUT I HAVE TO GO," AMELIA ANNOUNCES AFTER WE'VE raptly listened to Roxana detail the entire screening from beginning to end. "Joanna's not the only one who needs to cram for that precalc test. Math used to be one of my strong suits, but something about this year is already kicking my ass."

"Right? They really weren't kidding about junior year," I say.

"No, sir, they were not."

"Good luck," Roxana tells Amelia.

"Thanks," Amelia says brightly, and turns to me. But before I let her open her mouth and be the brave one again, I smile at her.

"I'll talk to you later," I say.

Her smile grows wider. "Okay. See you guys!" She gives Roxana and Devin a jaunty wave and touches me quickly on the shoulder, where I can feel that small jolt again even through my T-shirt. I watch as she joins the stream of people heading toward the exit.

"Where are Samira and the rest?" Roxana asks.

"They went to a screening of a new TV show," I say. "I think it lets out at five. So in about forty-five minutes," I conclude after glancing at my watch.

"Got it. So . . . what should we do?" Roxana asks.

Devin whips out his phone, brings up the NYCC app, and starts skimming through the schedule. "There's something called How to Survive a Zombie Apocalypse. Or Harry Potter Wand Duels."

"Oooh. Let me see that." Roxana stands at Devin's elbow, her face practically in the crook of his arm, as they read his small screen together.

I'm the third wheel. The thought comes unbidden. And as much as I've been fighting it this weekend, it's the truth and I have to accept it. Devin hasn't been tagging along, unwelcome, this whole time; Roxana has clearly wanted him around, has been returning all his attentions. I don't want to think about Roxana and Devin alone together at Comic Con, finding shared interests, falling in love, or—God forbid—kissing. But I also can't prevent it by being that awkward other presence. That's the first step, right? The admission? So I admit it, Devin. I can't win.

"Hey, guys. I think I'll just meet you in front of the *Mr. Advantageous* screening room at five. I actually want to get some work done," I say.

"Work?" Roxana asks, looking confused.

"Yeah, I just got an idea for an issue and I really have to write it down before I lose it. You know how I am." And that part is totally true. She does know that when an idea comes to me, I have to find a pen, or an iPad, or anything just to jot down at least a few words, or else I'll never see the thought again. How many times has Roxy seen me bend over in class, suddenly much more into my notebook than chemistry would ever inspire? Or stop midsentence during a conversation to open up the Notes app on my phone? In a way, this is one of those times. I realized it as I said it to her. I do need to write, not an issue necessarily, but . . . something.

"I think that room we were in with the raffle is empty now," I continue, "so I can duck in there to concentrate."

"Do you want me to come with you?" Roxana asks. "So we can talk it out?" She sounds weirdly eager, as if she really does want to come with me, as opposed to finally getting more alone time with Devin.

I shake my head. "Nah. I'm in that initial headspace thing. I'll discuss it with you later, though."

She stares at me, looking bizarrely shaken. "Of course you will." Her words almost sound menacing. Or is it threatened? I can't tell.

"Of course," I agree. "See you soon."

I turn and walk down the hallway, finally alone with my thoughts and ready to face them too. I'm right about the raffle room. It's not being used for anything official, but other people had the same idea I did. There are a few groups taking a break from the grind of the con, sitting on the floor and chatting. Other people are quietly typing or swiping on their laptops and phones. There are three outlets around the room, and those seem to have the most people congregated around them, charging up their various essential devices.

I find myself a nice bit of unoccupied carpet near a quiet section of wall, and I sit down. I take a few deep breaths, and then I open up my backpack and take out my worn stenographer's notebook and a pen. I flip through the filled pages—some packed with wisps of ideas that never turned into anything and some crammed with full outlines of *Mage High* issues—until I find the first empty page. I poise my pen at the top of it and I let my mind formulate the first thought: **"It's where I keep my selfness,"** Althena explained to Charlie in the very first issue.

Then I press the pen down, letting the words come out as they may.

"I've been thinking about Althena's green ear," I write. "How there are things that even a shape-shifting alien can't change about herself. There are things I can't change about myself, either. I'm always going to have fallen madly in love, for the very first time, at sixteen. And I know, even now, that will be a part of my selfness for always."

I write out my jumble of conflicting emotions. Every feeling I can think of that has come to pass this weekend: from jealousy to determination to crushing disappointment to unexpected elation. I write about dashed hopes and the element of surprise, how life makes you certain that you're headed down one path, only to push you through a secret door just as you think you can glimpse your oasis. How things hinge on an instantaneous decision, shifting your future like that topsy-turvy room in *Inception*.

And then, before I know it, I'm starting a character sketch. A new character for *Mage High*. A character who comes in brokenhearted, a transfer to the school who has lost his first love because of his (yet-to-be-determined) powers. He feels guilty and distraught. To the outside world, this makes him seem brooding and mysterious. Which, as any comics fan will tell you, is the perfect formula for an irresistible new superhero.

I make him an orphan because, well, I can't make him be *exactly* like me without it getting too weird. He won't have red hair, either, or be a total geek. But I also know he'll probably be a more complex character because of some of the things I've just gone through. Isn't that what writers are supposed to do? Gather life experience so that they can channel them and create great art? Isn't that what Zinc did when his writing career was going nowhere?

I'm just trying to brainstorm what my new character's fortified magical power could be when a shadow falls across the white spaces of my notebook. It's a familiar shadow. Even before I look up, I know it's Roxana. And she's alone.

"How's it going?" she asks as she looks down at me.

I glance at my notebook page. It's almost full. Then I flip back and realize I've filled over three pages with quick, excited handwriting. "Good," I tell her. "It's kinda flowing."

"It looks like it."

I move to stand up and realize my legs have fallen asleep from being stretched out in front of me, inert, for I don't even know how long. When I finally get up, I stamp my feet a little to get the blood flowing.

"Graham, why did you do it?" Roxana asks me quietly.

I look down at her. "Do what?" But then suddenly I know. She wants to know why I told her what I did last night. I sigh. It's not like I haven't spent the past day asking myself the same question. This conversation was always going to happen.

But then she surprises me. "Why did you let me have the ticket to the Zinc screening?"

I'm taken aback. *This* conversation I was not expecting, because the answer seems so obvious. "It would've felt wrong to be there without you, so I'd just rather you had it," I say. "Does that really surprise you?"

She's slow to answer. "That's the thing," she finally says. "It doesn't surprise me at all. But I'm in the screening, watching Althena and Noth meet. And their story is beginning, just like we both know it does, and it struck me—I swear right as her spaceship struck Earth—why doesn't it surprise me? Why do I always expect you to be so kind, to put me first, to be the greatest friend? It's like I take you for granted." She's staring straight into my eyes, like she's really searching for her answer there.

"I don't think you do," I say truthfully. "You're a great friend too, you know. My best friend."

But she shakes her head. "I asked myself if the roles were reversed, if I would have given up my ticket for you. And . . . I don't know. I honestly couldn't say I would." She finally looks down at her feet. "That's so selfish," she admits.

"Can you honestly say you wouldn't?"

She thinks about it. "I guess not," she finally mutters.

I smile down at her. "So there you are. Maybe you're not selfish. Maybe you'd be just as magnanimous as me," I tease, and manage to coax a small smile out of her. "For the record, I think you would have."

Her smile gets bigger. "Maybe you think I'm a better person than I really am. But either way, what you said was exactly right. It felt so wrong to be there without you."

"Let's make a pact." I stick my hand out. "Next time there's a Robert Zinc screening, we both win the raffle."

"Deal," she says, and shakes my hand. She squeezes it when we're done, taking a moment before she lets it go, like she's privately saying good-bye to something. Probably the same thing I'm going to be struggling to let go of for the next little while.

"So is it time to go meet everyone? I kinda lost track," I say as I glance at my watch. It's 4:45.

"Soon, but before we go, I want to talk about our bet."

"What bet?"

"The copper670 bet. Not Robert Zinc. Ergo, I win."

"Oh, right," I say, remembering. "So killing Slammerghini is out. Damn it."

"Looks like you'll be figuring out more creative ways for jail cells to come into play."

"'Tis my fate." I brace myself, suddenly suspicious. "Okay, so what is it we said you'd get? We're not killing off Spearfingers, are we?"

"I don't remember what I said then." She's staring up into my eyes again, and something in hers looks different. She looks intense, but other than that, I can't read her expression at all. It's like there's suddenly a facet of Roxy I don't know. "But what I really want is for you to forgive me. I want to say I'm so sorry for how I acted last night. And this morning."

I'm so taken aback again that I can't help but give a little laugh, probably out of sheer tension. "Oh, come on. That's a stupid thing to waste your bet on." I try to say it lightly.

She shakes her head. "It's not. It's the most vital thing there is. I can't stand to have you upset with me. I can't stand that I hurt you. . . ." Her voice breaks and, speaking of things that can't be stood, I'm worried that she's going to start to cry.

"Roxy," I begin gently. "There's nothing to forgive. I'm not upset. Well, I am, but I'm not mad at you. It's, you know . . . complicated."

"Yes," she says. "But I reacted badly. I was just so . . ."

"Shocked?" I help her out.

She nods. "Yes. Though maybe I shouldn't have been. But the thought of losing our friendship is beyond terrifying. Because it's the most important thing to me. Because *you* are the most important thing." She gently takes my hand. "I love you, you know."

I smile weakly down at her. "I know. Just not in that way."

She looks down at our hands and shakes her head. "I don't know. I don't know in what way I love you. It's just . . . the Graham way." She looks back up at me. "Thirty years from now, I want you to be in my life. I don't know if Devin will be there. Or any other guy. But you . . . I can't imagine *you* not being there."

I take a deep breath as I gaze at her, and though the breath catches in my throat, it eventually releases, and a part of me is released with it. I bring her hand to my lips, and I kiss it gently. And then I let it go.

"I will be, Roxana," I promise. "We will be okay." I realize it's what everyone from Felicia to Samira has told me—in one way, shape, or form—this weekend, and I also realize that it's true. Broken hearts mend—if my dad isn't living proof of that, I don't know what is. And I'm lucky, in a way, because I still get to have Roxana in my life every day and, hopefully, for a long time.

I feel there's only one thing left to say. "Writing session on Tuesday?"

Roxy nods, her eyes unmistakably filled with tears this time. "Yes. Please," she croaks out.

"I think I may have figured out a new character," I say as I make a show of gathering my stuff, letting Roxy wipe her eyes in some semblance of privacy.

"Really? Is that what you were doing here?" she says after a moment, gesturing to the notebook I'm putting away in my backpack.

I nod. "Still wrapping my head around some of the details. But Tuesday. We'll definitely talk."

"Tuesday," she repeats, with a small, relieved laugh, and she rubs at her face some more and takes a deep breath before speaking again. "And actually, there's something very important that I need to show you. I assume you haven't been on Twitter?" She takes out her phone and starts scrolling.

"Not lately," I reply, puzzled.

"Presented without commentary," she says as she holds her phone out to me.

It's open to a profile page: @robert_zinc. It has a little blue check mark next to it that means it's been verified. It already has 83,458 followers. And there's just one tweet there and it's from a couple of hours ago.

"I like this kid's style . . . ," it says, followed by a retweet of a video tagged with #InigoMontoyaSmackdown.

"Oh . . . my . . . God . . . Is this . . . this can't be . . ." I cannot formulate sentences. I can just stare down at the glowing screen in my hand like I'm a time traveler who has never seen a smartphone before.

The grin on Roxana's face could not get any bigger. "Oh, yes. That is really Robert Zinc. Tweeting. And his first missive to the masses is *about you*."

I look up at her. "A hoax?" I croak out.

She shakes her head triumphantly. "Nope, I don't think so." She watches me silently freak out for another second before she says, "You do realize what this means, right? That in some small way . . . *Robert Zinc knows who you are.*"

Dear Internet. I love you. Hard.

It's the only thought I can formulate.

Roxana gives me another couple of minutes alone with the screen before she touches my hand with a laugh. "All right, Internet sensation Graham Posner. Shall we go find the others?"

I look up at her and slowly nod, finally handing her phone back, my hands still a little shaky.

"Anything in particular you want to check out now?" she asks. "I think there are some post-NYCC events happening in the neighborhood."

I shake my head, dazed and also realizing that I still honestly don't have much of an idea of today's schedule. I clear my throat and test out regular speech again. "Let's meet up with the group," I manage to say. "And then we'll take a consensus."

"So . . . whatever Casey has in his spreadsheet?" Roxy teases.

"Pretty much. Speaking of which," I say as I shoulder my backpack, realizing I have something to tell her, too. "What would you think if I put the names Casey Zucker and Felicia Obayashi in a sentence together?"

"Um . . . smartest kids in our class?" Roxana responds with a perplexed shrug.

"Mmm-hmm," I say, and then I waggle my eyebrows.

"Wait. What? No," Roxana sputters, and then she clearly starts racking her brain. "Oh my gosh. Really?"

I put my hands up. "I have no confirmation of anything. Just my own astute observations over the past couple of days."

"Oh my God. Do you really think . . . holy crap. It kinda makes sense. In an insane way."

"Yeah, in an insane their-kids-would-dominate-the-universe way. Talk about supergenes . . ."

"They would be mutants. Actual, honest-to-goodness mutants."

As we start to leave the room, my phone buzzes in my pocket, and I take it out to see a text from Amelia. **Have you seen Twitter?!**

I grin at it before typing out a quick response and catching up with Roxana in the hallway, where we join a throng of superheroes and villains. But for once, I see all those characters and I don't really envy them their fantasy worlds. I'm okay with my reality, as messy and imperfect as it may be. I don't really know what comes next, but honestly, isn't that the best part of writing a story anyway?

Maybe it's the best part of real life, too.

Acknowledgments

I'm so grateful to my spectacular editor, Zareen Jaffery, who championed this book, Graham, and me from the very beginning. My fandom for you knows no bounds. I think I need to start an entire forum dedicated to the enormous talents of Lucy Ruth Cummins, Dolly Faibyshev, and Tim Sundholm, for this astonishingly perfect cover that brings Graham to glorious life. All the heart emojis go to the wonderful team at Simon & Schuster that I am so lucky to work with: Ksenia Winnicki, Mekisha Telfer, Justin Chanda, Anne Zafian, Jenica Nasworthy, Katy Hershberger, Chrissy Noh, and KeriLee Horan. And, of course, the gushiest of valentines to my agent, Victoria Marini.

More than anything I've written before, this book was shaped and guided by some of the world's best beta readers. First and foremost, I must thank Billy Henehan for sharing his extensive Comic Con knowledge and stories with me (and for inspiring me to start attending the convention in the first place). And Sarah Skilton, who helped me find the story's true ending when I couldn't see it for myself. I don't think this book would really exist without the two of you. Thank you so much also to Julie Henehan, Katie Blackburn, and Jenny Goldberg, for helping me through my narrative dilemma with their invaluable and astute feedback.

As any nerd worth their salt knows, geek minutiae is *very* serious stuff, and I would like to thank some experts who helped me with some of those very important details: Andrew Lobel, Gina Rosati, and Jerry Rosati. Thank you to Nicholas Doyle for writing a real-life (and spectacular) version of "Something on the Quiet." And so much amused gratitude to Dave Henehan for cosplaying as Graham at NYCC last year.

Thank you to Nora Ephron, Cameron Crowe, Amy Heckerling, and, of course, John Hughes, for a lifetime worth of inspiration and honest, romantic, unforgettable stories. Thank you to the Killers for music to write to and dream by.

I'm so grateful to my mom for all her enthusiasm and support throughout the years and for babysitting so that I could write. Which leads me to thank my darling son, who outraced this book out into the world, and my husband, Graig. I love you both up all the hidden staircases in Hogwarts . . . and back.